Reaper

By
Ivan Navi

Illustrations
By
Kiyoichi

Edited
By
Yosuke Imagawa

Copyright © 2016 Ivan Navi.
Illustrations by Kiyoichi.

All rights reserved. Without limiting rights under the copyright reserved above, no part of this publication may be reproduced, stored, introduced into a retrieval system, distributed or transmitted in any form or by any means, including without limitation photocopying, recording, or other electronic or mechanical methods, without the prior written permission of the publisher, except in the case of brief quotations embodied in critical reviews and certain other noncommercial uses permitted by copyright law. The scanning, uploading, and/or distribution of this document via the internet or via any other means without the permission of the publisher is illegal and is punishable by law. Please purchase only authorized editions and do not participate in or encourage electronic piracy of copyrightable materials.

This is a work of fiction. Names, characters, businesses, places, events, and incidents are either the products of the author's imaginations or used in fictitious manner. Any resemblance to actual persons, living or dead, or actual events is purely coincidental.

Bronte took a deep breath, "Do or die, then? How can I refuse such an invitation?"

Chapter 04: Light And Shadows

Table of Contents

Chapter 01: Vacation From Death — 1

Chapter 02: Sofi — 12

Chapter 03: Pax — 27

Chapter 04: Light And Shadows — 55

Chapter 05: Into The Dark — 74

Chapter 06: Talbot — 88

Chapter 07: Lightning Of The Gods — 94

Chapter 08: A Deathless World — 110

Chapter 09: Life — 125

Chapter 10: Deatz — 131

Afterword — 143

Chapter 01: Vacation From Death

The world is a complicated and strange place that is filled with strange things. People are different from one another and this gives the world all the variety of differences that make it so complex. Still, there are things that are the same all over. There is one idea that seems to be found in every culture, the soul.

Some would argue that it is only the case because of the shared unconscious mind that people are said to have. Maybe that is the case and maybe it's not.

Along with the soul there is a figure that is said to take the soul of the dead to their final resting place. Some people call these figures Psychopomps or Angels of Death or Guides to the Afterlife, but most people today call them Reapers.

In Ancient Egypt, they had Anubis, the Aztecs had Xolotl, in Celtic stories they have Dullahan, in Norse Mythology there were the Valkyrie and there is a modern cloaked figure known as the Grim Reaper. A quick internet search would get you a very long list of figures who are said to carry the souls of the dead to wherever they go.

Each reaper has a basic set of skills and a specialty when it come to collecting souls. There are reapers who are motherly and loving as your own mother and they go to children who have died. These reapers tend to these children and hold them and ease them away from fear like a good mother would. Even after having to tend to millions of children in such states they never lose that compassion and always smile to any child who needs to see a smiling face.

There are reapers that look like animals out of myth and fantasy that come to children who die so quick they don't even notice they've died. These reapers play with the children and give them one last glorious day and ease them into accepting their deaths like lulling them to their sleep.

There are reapers that are monsters that hunt down the souls who refuse to move on, souls that ravished the world in life and would continue to do so in death. These reapers grab twisted and horrid souls and drag them to the afterlife they've earned.

There are reapers that like to play games with people. They go to people who won't accept they are dead just like that and they play a game with them to decide what happens next.

There are reapers soaked in blood who wear scars like badges of honor. They are reapers that go to the warriors who refuse to leave. These reapers give the warriors one last battle and by fighting, they let the warriors have their peace.

Normally when someone dies and they accept their fate and they move on to an afterlife or get reincarnated. One way or another the reaper gets the person to accept that they had died and they embrace their death. At that moment Death embraces them and takes them to the next part of their journey. Every reaper knows of Death and knows why Death created them. Death will at one point meet every living thing in the cosmos, but some refuse to go to this meeting or aren't ready for it, that's why the reapers were made to get them there. Then there is Pax.

Pax is a rather unimpressive reaper. Reapers can look like anything or anyone they want, but Pax chooses to look like a pale man in his twenties with dark and messy hair. Pax is a little on the thin side and a little too tall to look like an average man. He wore a plain black suit with matching tie and black tie that he left a little loose. Not to say he wasn't attractive some women and men had called him pretty, mostly due to his brilliant blue eyes and good cheek bones.

Pax deals with souls that are just confused and who have made mistakes, big mistakes. Some would say that his very nature is mistakes, that idea has gotten to him after centuries of work. It has worn away at his spirit and he's not the most eager reaper. He does his work and he does it well and treats each spirit with respect and with all the delicacy they require. Still Pax isn't one hundred percent pleased with his state of existence.

At that moment he was waiting in a dimension the reapers had come to call the waiting room. Often spirits of the dead crossed into the afterlives through that dimension, but really it was where the reapers rested between assignments if they didn't have anything else to do. The dimension was a world to itself virtually endless and shaped by the general will and desires of the reapers present.

The small portion of the world had been turned into a small food court and Pax sat down by a table. Pax slowly sipped a glass of lemonade. Reapers really didn't need to eat or drink, but he found it peaceful.

A sweet and sugary voice spoke behind him. "You're acting like a moody teenager again."

"What?" Pax turned around to find another reaper standing there. "Valdis? What are you doing here?"

Valdis was a reaper that Pax had known for centuries, one far older than he was but chose to look much younger. Valdis looked like a fourteen year old girl with long silvery hair done up in twin pig tails. Valdis had emerald green eyes that sometimes seemed to glimmer. Valdis wore a red tie over a black dress shirt and a red plaid skirt. To complete her outfit she had on a long black coat. Though there wasn't any rule that said reapers needed to wear black they tended to like that color.

Valdis was a reaper who collected the souls of heroes. Pax never said it, but he thought she had a more dignified version of his job. Pax could understand people making big mistakes, but centuries of witnessing them all was a little much.

"What are you doing here?" Pax asked dryly.

She pouted at him, "Well, that's not a very polite greeting."

"Sorry about that." Pax quickly apologized. "I'm just wondering what you're doing here."

Valdis smiled and sat across from him, "I was looking for you. Upper management has a message for you. They've been trying to tell you, but you haven't been making it easy to be found."

"I didn't have anyone I had to collect so I was just trying to rest a little."

"Well, it does seem like you are going to have some time to rest." Valdis grinned at him speaking with a flowery voice.

"What are you talking about?"

"It's your turn to have some time off, you are to take a vacation."

"I thought I had one a decade ago."

"No, that was me. I had a wonderful time traveling through Italy trying all those tasty dishes." Valdis smiled at the memories.

"Of course it would have to be about food with you." Pax rolled her eyes. He was half certain that every moment she had off, she spent it trying to taste test any food that caught her eye.

"Now let's go." Valdis waved him on. "Or else-"

The world around them blended together into an endless blackness before it was replaced by a stone room. Its design was ancient and was more than fitting to call it a tomb. The room was lit with torches that besides giving the room light, and it seemed to give the room a little warmth. The walls had Ancient Egyptian hieroglyphs scrawled onto them. At the end of the room loomed a tall and imposing figure. It was a half man, half jackal. His body was certainly shaping like a man, but his head was clearly that of a jackal. Black fur covered his body and his body was covered with a white ceremonial robe.

With a booming voice he said simply, "Pax."

"Or else they will bring us here." Valdis said, looking up to the man finishing her sentence. "Hello Anubis." Valdis smiled greeting him. "I had just found Pax and was about to bring him here."

Pax had fallen backwards when they were moved, but when he saw Anubis, he jumped onto his feet. Anubis was one of the oldest living reapers and one that commanded great respect. Though most days now he spent helping keep order with the younger reapers, he still collected the occasional soul. It was thought that any soul collected by the higher ups was of great importance.

The jackal's nose twitched as he looked at Pax, "Pax, it is your time to take a break from your duties as a reaper."

Pax stood straight almost like a soldier in front of a drill sergeant even if a little lax, "It's my turn for the vacation."

"Do not take it so casually." The elder reaper spoke. "It is no mere vacation, but a process we must all go through. You will be transformed into a mortal like state. Only living will you understand the hearts and minds of those we offer passage. The price of life is death and only by living you can understand what that means." Anubis pulled out a small black leather wallet and held it out. "Take it."

"Do I have to?" Pax sighed, "It always feels so strange."

"Take it." Anubis' voice was steady but forceful.

Pax took the wallet in his hand and silvery light exploded out of it and engulfed him. He let out a yell and started to breath heavily. "Always feels weird." Pax groaned. "Now what?"

"Live." Anubis said simply.

"Oh, I have a perfect place to go." Valdis chirped. "I can send you there."

Pax had no objections or any preferences so he nodded his agreement, "Fine, where are you sending me?"

Valdis smiled brightly before giving him a wink, "That's a surprise. Just have some fun and I will check up on you later."

The gentle touch was all that it took and the world faded around him and was replaced by a bustling city. A gentle summer breeze swept past his skin. He took a breath and let the air into his lungs. It's the little thing he didn't notice as a reaper thing like feeling the warm breeze. He had been turned into human in almost every aspect. Most of his powers were gone except his ability to communicate in any language and that was mostly left in as a tool when the reapers were left to explore. Pax was stuck in the form unable to change his appearance and he couldn't teleport at the blink of an eye. Pax could no longer make himself invisible but the moment no one seemed to have notice him suddenly appear. He was still amazed how humanity could often ignore such fantastic things that were just hiding beneath their noses.

    At the moment Pax was trying to figure out where he was. The city did look familiar, but having visited every city for the last few hundred years they started to blur together. The architecture certainly had a western feel to it and somewhat classical so he assumed he was somewhere in Europe. He found himself walking through some sort of marketplace that was buzzing with people, he could make out people speaking German, but that only narrowed it down to a few counties.

    That was when a smell wafted over him, it was the smell of rich chocolate. It was sweet and strong and it made his mouth water. His eyes fell to a small shop where freshly baked pastries filled the air with their sweet smell only for it to mix with the smell of rich teas and coffees.

    "Sachertorte." Pax said as he spotted the small chocolate cake. "She sent me to Vienna, Austria."

    The Sachertorte was a small chocolate sponge cake with an apricot jam and a dark chocolate icing. Just looking at the cake Pax couldn't help but think how the cake would taste.

    "Of course she would send me here." Pax shook his head. Pax had known Vienna as a city rich with history, culture and wondrous music, but Valdis had sent him there to try a signature pastry, even one so tasty looking. Valdis would spend her free time trying out snacks and food all over the world, even though she had no real need to eat. Now it looked like Valdis had just sent him on a vacation centered on cake to do the same.

    Pax sighed a little annoyed by her actions, but decided to make the best of it, he'd be there for about a week before he'd regain his powers and be able to move anywhere on a whim. He looked down to his hand where the black wallet remained. The wallet was a tool left to the reaper that would create any identification or money they needed, it would allow them to blend into the world like any other human.

    "I guess I should at least get lunch." Pax said as he realized hunger was making his stomach growl.

Pax went inside and ordered himself a slice of the cake and a black coffee. He sat down and enjoyed his small meal as he watched the world pass him by. The cake was delicious, practically melting in his mouth. As he slowly took in his simple meal he watched the world pass before him. He wondered if that was just him or all reapers, to find an interest in just observing the world but not truly interacting with it. Valdis certainly jumped in when it came to food. In ancient time Anubis was practically welcomed into people's houses. Some reapers were welcomed and accepted and some had become revered in legends. Pax didn't think he would ever become one like that and in all honesty he didn't want to. He didn't know what he wanted from his existence.

Overall that would have been a quiet and uninteresting afternoon if it had continued like that, but it didn't. For reasons that Pax didn't understand at that moment everyone in the shop got up and left the shop all at once. It wasn't as if an alarm had rung out or someone told them to do that. Pax got up, looked around and noticed other stores and shops had emptied into the streets. The streets themselves had become filled with people just leaving the area.

If you were in the area watching this you'd probably wouldn't be watching them leave but also leaving. Pax stood in the middle of the street as it quickly emptied and was left utterly confused as why it was happening.

Pax like most reapers had been around for centuries and had seen many strange things and learned about things most people couldn't even imagine. He scratched his head, trying to make sense of it. Pax took a breath and started to calmly observe the area and the situation. Nothing seemed to be different than any other area except that now it was empty. Something was affecting people and only people as he could still hear the birds chirping and he had no urge to walk away, he was almost human, but still had his reaper essence with a tiny bit of power. That was when he noticed the hairs on the back of his neck stand up, that was when he felt a wave of energy pass over him. It wasn't anything dramatic just a small touch of power flowing through the air in the area.

"Magic." Pax mumbled to himself.

Magic was known to the reapers and even some of them had learned to use it. Reapers and humans could both learn to detect the presence of such energies, but it took some awareness to do it. It didn't take him much more to assume that someone had used magic to just nudge people away from the area. He had often heard that there were spells to keep people away from certain area where people would perform magical rituals and things like that. From what he could understand about it after the spell faded or was removed everyone would return never really realizing that had all left.

Pax let out a sigh deciding if he should just leave the area or finish his coffee. As he was deep in his own thoughts so much so that he didn't notice the silence as all the birds left the area.

He also didn't notice a woman yelling,

"Help!"

She was desperate and scared as she ran towards the only person who she saw. She placed her hand on his shoulder grabbing his attention and Pax flinched as he felt a spark like static electricity run between them. Pax looked at her trying to get some idea of who she was. She wore a simple, light green dress and long white gloves. Her long dark hair framed her heart shape face. Her bright green eyes shone brightly on her face. Her skin was smooth and pale with a pinkish hue. She was breathing hard as she tried to catch her breath and tears threaten to form at the edge of her eyes.

"Help." She said breathlessly.

Pax turned to her and their eyes meet, but the second their eyes locked on one another her body tensed and she flinched. She pulled away and backed away slowly. Her eyes were wide and filled with shock.

"W-what are you?" she spoke with a soft voice.

"What?" Pax replied, unsure what she meant.

The air grew colder and large dark clouds filled the sky

above them. That was when Pax realized something, he only noticed one wave of energy and that happened after everyone left so that meant that another spell was triggered a moment ago.

"Is he a friend of yours?" Pax asked as he pointed to a cloaked figure at the end of the road he had just spotted.

The woman looked back, "He found me."

The sound of lightning cracked as a bolt of electricity struck the ground before them shattering the road. It was loud enough that nearby shop windows shattered. The cloaked figure snickered to himself.

The last hit sent both the woman and Pax back and from what Pax could tell she had been knocked out. He moaned as he felt the bruises starting to form where some of the rocks had hit his body when dislodged from the ground. Pax wished he could just teleport or turn invisible, but he knew he couldn't.

"Why didn't you go?" The man said in Greek.

Pax didn't think he was supposed to understand him, but being that language was one of his remaining powers he really didn't have a choice. He spoke in Greek. "Oh, so that was your trick."

"You understand me? It is a shame really more reason I can't let you live. Everyone in the cabal has very strict orders not to let anyone know anything about us and here you've gone and seen me and the girl."

"I am having a really unlucky day."

"So it would seem." He smirked under his cloak. He started to whisper an ancient prayer to the god Zeus, the king of the Olympian gods and master of lightning.

Pax felt the energies moving and shifting urging the lighting and forcing it down and directing it. It wasn't like natural lighting were the forces of nature moved it to the ground this was being forced and it would be slower but still very fast. Pax took a breath, feeling the energy about to erupt and fall on him. He jumped over to the woman's body and covered her with his own as closed his eyes. He felt heat coming towards him and even with his eyes closed he saw the white light as the lightning was being called down.

It was a crack, a very loud crack, one that was made when the lightning hit the ground with a lot of force. It was like a small explosion shattering the stones of the road and turning it into dust. The magician waved his hand blowing the dust away.

"No..." he said in shock.

The crater where the lightning hit was empty except for broken stones.

"Where is the girl?" He said in confusion as he looked around, but the magician saw no sign of Pax or the woman.

In an alley nearby Pax sighed in relief as he carried the woman away. He didn't know if he was lucky or he actually had some sort of skill. The fake lighting was slower, but not much so, when he saw the white light, he pushed the woman away just barely managing to escape the brunt of the attack. When the blast kicked up some dust he quickly got up and carried her away and hid in an alley.

Pax had an idea of human psychology after watching them for years, if the magician needed the girl he'd be in a panic for some time until he realized he hadn't actually vaporized her. By that time they could get away and hide. So weak and hurt, he carried her away deeper into the city and away from the man who tried to blast them. All the time asking him if it was a mistake to get involved and risk getting hurt. As a reaper, many people had begged him to let them live and it seemed like they never got the response they wanted. Maybe this once he could help. She asked for his help and for once he felt he could do something.

Only time would tell if it truly was a mistake.

Chapter 02: Sofi

Her head hurt, it hurt as much as you'd expect it to hurt after hitting the hard ground. She forced her eyes open. She didn't know where she was or what had happened. She found herself resting on something soft and as she took in the room she was in she realized she was in the bed of a fancy hotel.

"Wow, you guys work fast." A voice spoke up from the doorway.

She raised her head and saw the same pale man from before walking out an old man to the door.

The other man wore a vest and had a tape measure around his neck.

The pale man took out a black wallet and several bills out of. Handing the money over, "Thank you for your work. I can't even see the rips in my suit."

The man was clearly a tailor and he simply smiled to the kind words, "I do love my work."

Pax smiled at the old man and handed him a few more bills as a bonus before the tailor left.

Pax turned around fiddling with his jacket before he turned his eyes to the girl. "Oh, you are up."

She looked at him confused.

"You do understand me, right? I'm never really sure what language I speak. All these years and I've never really stopped to think about it. I sort of just start speaking to whatever is appropriate. You know, I speak to whatever my listener can understand."

"You're speaking German, an Austrian dialect, you were but you slipped into Hungarian and then some Estonian when you started to speak to me."

"Oh, so you speak those." Pax asked her.

"My family moved a lot and I've picked up a number of languages over time."

Pax was sure she switched into Ukrainian to see if he could follow. He didn't have to think about it, he just switched languages, he actually had to focus on what he was speaking to know which language he switched to.

"I think I know you a little better, but I still don't know your name." Pax moved closer to her.

She pulled back the instant he moved towards her.

Pax decided to go first trying to reassure her that he meant no harm, "My name is Pax."

"Sofi, my name is Sofi."

"That's a nice name." Pax said, putting on his best reassuring smile. Pax found this whole situation wasn't so different from greeting a newly dead spirit. "I have some questions for you."

"I have some questions for you too."

"So let's start with that. You looked at me and asked what I was."

"You're not human, are you?" Sofi said timidity entering her voice.

"No, normally I'm not. You caught me on a special day."

Sofi stared at him in a mixture of awe and wonder. "I've seen something like you before."

"Like what? When?"

"I was in a car, with my parents, I couldn't be older than five when it happened."

"What happened?"

"There was an accident on the road, the roads were all wet from the rain and the car slid off the road. I was the only one that survived." Sofi looked off in the distance recalling the old memory. "There was a man there. I was hurt and they told me I was imaging things, but I know what I saw. A man with huge black wings picked up my parents from the wreck. He was beautiful like an angel. He told them things and let them say goodbye to me. He told them that I couldn't hear them, but they should just say it, but I did hear them and I saw him. The thing is I could see them trapped in the car too. They were in two places but the ones in the car with me were just bodies and what I was seeing were... well, their souls."

"Thanatos, it sounds like Thanatos." Pax said in a casual manner. "That pretty boy likes being compared to angels." Pax scoffed at the idea even though, let's face it, he's a pretty boy too. "He goes to people who are all but ready to accept death as a natural part of life, but they have a connection they need to let go off. Something to say goodbye to."

"You are like him." Sofi said, her eyes slowly widening.

"Yes, he's a reaper and so am I, except I'm on vacation and was turned human."

"You really aren't human?"

"Not at all. Reapers just tend to look like humans most of the time."

"Reapers as in grim reaper? That skeleton figure with the cloak and scythe from those folk tales that traveled around Europe collected the dead during the Black Plague? That Grim Reaper?"

"Oh, don't get me started on that guy, that show off. Yes, we are the people that help the dead move on when they aren't ready to head to the next stage. The thing is you shouldn't be able to see us when we're with the spirits, you shouldn't even be able to see spirits. How did you do that? And why was that magician after you?"

"Magicians? Like in wizards?"

"Well, magicians are normal people who learn magic and wizards are males who have a natural talent to use magic." Pax just shook his head. "I take it that's not the point. Why was he chasing you?"

"I've been apart of a small traveling circus for a few years now. We travel around Europe performing and doing shows and I would just have a small tent where I perform readings. I can just know things about people by looking at them or touching them. I can't actually see the future, I just tell them enough about their past that they believe whatever I tell them about the future. It is just all about having a little fun. It was a fun life."

"So what happened then?" Pax had heard enough stories to know that things just don't jump from happy eccentric life to running away just like that.

"We were in Belgium setting up for another show when that man showed up. I looked at him and I saw something I hadn't seen before. I didn't know it at the time, but I think it was magic. Whatever thing lets him use magic, I was seeing him and seeing things I had never seen before. I also saw his nature, there were desire and loneliness. I saw that he wanted to take me and he was under strict orders to do so by something that scared him. I excused myself to use the bathroom and crawled out the window as soon as I could. I spent days hitchhiking and hiding away on trains trying to lose him over the country borders."

"So what happened today?"

"He caught up and he looked serious and he even wore that cloak and no one seemed to notice him. He started to chant something to some small statue and everyone just left and I ran trying to lose him in the alleys when I ran into you."

"You never found out why he wants you?"

"No, but I'm guessing it was my power. It's the only thing special about me."

"How does it work anyway?"

"I'm not sure. I've never figured it out. I just look at people when they get close to them I know about them. I know if they are kind and if I can trust them. I know if people are hurt and if they are trying to hide something. I can tell if they're not human apparently. Do you know what I am?"

"I don't know. I've been around a lot time and seen a lot of strange things but I don't know. I mean there are people born with gifts, some see the future, some see the past, some can read minds, some can move things with their minds and there are magical artifacts scattered everywhere with things most people can't dream of. There are people working on things that you would only think was possible in science fiction books. There are thing from other worlds, worlds from high above and worlds that are so close you could almost reach out and touch them."

Sofi leaned in eager to hear more, she had thought of her whole life that she was something that didn't belong with the rest of the normal world, but now someone was telling her that she was just a small part of a much larger world. For the first time she felt that there could actually be a place for her somewhere out there for her. For the first time since her parents died, she didn't feel so alone.

She stayed silent, letting the weight of everything sink in. Her heart raced with excitement at the implications.

"So what now?" Sofi asked for the man that gave her hope.

"Well, I'm going to help you get somewhere safe." Pax told her calmly. "I'm not so sure about this hotel. They have a tailor on staff and didn't give me too many odd looks when I carried an unconscious girl in with me. They also exchanged money for me. I have a suitcase filled with money from all over Europe. I can help you get somewhere safe."

"Where? Switzerland?"

"If you like. I made enough money that you could buy a castle."

"You can make money?" Sofi was surprised by that.

"Upper management gave me something that can give me documents and money so I don't have to worry about getting by. I think we have to leave as soon as possible. The magician might try something and I'm just not sure what, it would be best to put some distance between us and him."

"Thank you." Sofi looked at him with tears of joy forming in her eyes. "Thank you." Sofi moved forwards and hugged him. "Thank you."

* * * *

Far away the magician sat down at a cafe, he had removed the cloak and tried his best to blend in. His name was Bronte and he had grown up near some old ruins in Greece. As a child, he used to take tourist to the ruins to make some money. One night just for fun and boredom, he decided to climb up to one of the old ruins. It was the middle of the night and he hadn't expected anyone but he found a small cabal. The cabal was made up of people who still worshipped the ancient gods and were holding a ritual to call on the power of the gods. That was his first experience with real magic and he got them to show him how they did it. They taught him a lot, they could have taught him some more ethics, but they never got around to it. Bronte was an orphan and didn't have anything, what little money he had he fought for and it was the only thing that kept him alive. The magicians gave him something even greater.

Bronte shook off the memories of the past and he started to remember everything he had done on this mission. He was supposed to bring the girl in to complete their goals. They had found where she was supposed to be but when he got close she ran. He tried to do a tracking spell, but he needed an item of hers that held great meaning to her, she wasn't materialistic and nothing she had carried any real emotional weight. He tried to use hairs but found none, she was far too clean to be normal.

She had no real home, she had been moving for most of her life so she never had a home. If she had, he could use it as a connection to her but that was just another option cut off from him. He had to use much more mundane methods to track her. He had to talk to people and find clues to which direction she was going all while avoid too much attention. It almost sounded fun to play the detective, but he found it much harder than it seemed in dramas.

He was lucky that his attack hadn't actually killed her. He felt like an idiot for spending ten minutes panicking. The only glimmer of hope he had found a piece of the road that fit in the palm of his hand. The only thing that made it special was a blood splatter on it. He wasn't sure whose blood it was, if it was the man or the woman he searched for but that didn't matter he was sure one would be with the other. With just the little blood, he could use it for a location spell and find the owner of the blood anywhere. At the moment the spell was set and the blood stains glowed faintly. The magician smirked and took a sip of coffee waiting to regain some of the energy he wasted on his foolish attacks. It wouldn't take long and he'd find her. The blood splatter glowed ever so slightly alerting him that they were on the move.

* * * *

Sofi scratched at the bandage on her forehead. They spent a few moments tending to her wound and bruises. They were in the lobby of the hotel and Pax was a short distance away talking to a man behind the counter. Pax was just getting some traveler information and a moment later walked to her carrying all sort sorts of brochures. Pax finished up at the counter and paid for the room and wandered over to her.

"Well, now we have to decide where to go?" Pax told her flatly. "I got information on trains to all over Europe, busses and even airplanes."

"Where would I be safe?"

"I don't know. Magic doesn't just stop working when you enter a new country. All I know is that we should get some distance between you and that magician."

"So where should we go?"

"I don't know. I really don't know how to help you. My best idea is to find another magician or a spell caster and get them to use a spell that keeps you hidden."

"Do you know someone who can do that?"

"No, the people I meet are usually dead and they're not helpful."

"Then let's go to the train station and get the first train out so at least we can put some distance between us and the guy that was chasing me. It will give us time to get some sort of idea of what to do."

So with that half a plan in hand, they decided to go to the train station. They took a taxi from the hotel to the train station.

The train station was a block-y modern looking building with huge mirror like windows that covered the whole side of the building. It glimmered like a crystal in the sunlight. Inside, the floors were cement and the walls glimmered with glass arts filled with shapes and colors, but otherwise it was like any other major train station.

Pax walked over to the board by the wall checking on the time for the next train out, To his disappointment, "It's not for another hour." Pax sighed as he told Sofi. "There are some local trains, but they won't get us far."

Left with no other options they bought the tickets and walked over to the area close to where the trains traveling long distance would depart. They didn't have anything that you'd call luggage as Pax didn't have anything and Sofi was forced to leave everything behind when she ran.

They sat on a bench and waited because that was all they could do. Pax fell into his old pattern and started to people watched. He noticed a young man wearing a dark hoodie sitting on a bench across from them with a pair of large orange head phone blocking out all sound for him and his head nodding to whatever song he heard. Pax watched as a woman in business attired paced nearby, staring at a clock. The young woman in casual clothing leaned against a wall seemingly waiting. Her long black hair was neatly pinned up. An old man sat on a nearby seat, seemingly fighting the urge to fall asleep. The old man tugged at his old worn out brown jacket every few moments as it was a blanket. Pax sighed noting how few people were there that day. The silence of the train station let the few footsteps they heard echo around them.

Sofi wrung her hands impatiently as she took a few sideways glances at the reaper that sat beside her. For almost her entire life she had the feeling that something had been waiting for her and now it looked like there it was. Her mind raced with hundreds of ideas and questions and she had the feeling that the reaper might have the answers.

Sofi decided to ask something simple, "You're a reaper, but you're a human right now?"

"Yes," Pax sighed a little. "My bosses think that making us human for a week every once in a while will make us more emphatic to the dead."

"And you don't like being human?"

"It's not bad, it's just a little inconvenient to suddenly need to do human things like eating...." Pax pushed down his sleeve at a bandage he was covering a slowly forming bruise. "And the wounds. It's one thing to watch humanity, but it's another thing to experience it."

"Isn't that the point of this whole thing?"

"Yes, I guess you're right." Pax found himself admitting the point. "It's just that it takes a lot to hurt a reaper so I'm not really used to pain."

Sofi let her hand trace the bandage on her forehead as she just remembered it, the pain had become dull and she forgot it but now she realized it wasn't the same for Pax. Sofi assumed it was something like how a baby not used to pain would cry out for the smallest thing.

Sofi couldn't help but ask, "Is there nothing you can do to stop these magicians?"

"No, I don't have much power in this form." Pax told her taking a glance at the clock. "With my full power I could go anywhere on the planet in a second, change my appearance, making it so people can't see me and so much more but now all I can do is to talk any language. I don't see what good I am."

Sofi tried to give him a reassuring smile, "I don't know about that. I feel a little safer with you around."

Pax only replied with a happy smile. "Thank you for saying that."

Sofi rubbed her tired eyes, "It has been a crazy day. I found out that magic is real and there are grim reapers."

"Is that such a surprise? I mean you have that whole weird power thing, you haven't run into anything strange since you've had it?"

"No, I've never run into anything supernatural. Everyone

I've met before you and that magician has seem perfectly normal."

"Is there no one in your family that has some weird gifts?"

"No, my parents were a little odd but never saw anything like this. I never knew anything about the rest of my family. I was taken in by a family friend who worked in the circus when I was a little girl. They took me in and everyone thought things I saw and felt was just a reaction to my parent's death. They all treated me like family and never judged me."

"They sound nice."

"They are and I had to leave without saying goodbye, I hope they're okay."

"And none of them were anything strange?"

"No, they are all plenty strange but nothing supernatural." Sofi scratched her chin curiously. "What else is out there? I know reapers and magicians are real, but what else?"

Pax ran his fingers through his hair as he thought, "There are all sorts of things. Spirits, fairies, shape shifters, dragons, ghouls, creatures that feed off fear, ghosts, psychics, dragons, werewolves, lizard people, seers, trolls-"

Sofi interrupted him, "And am I any of those?"

"I have no idea what you are. It's not any sort of mental power, it's like you can read people's essence and their past too. You can just know people. You can know what is there even if its hidden."

"I know who people are. They can't hide who they are to me. I can tell when they are lying. I just know them, I don't see why anyone would want me."

"Let's not stay and find out." Pax then noticed something, it was something small that most people would have just ignored, the woman looked at them and the second she saw him looking at her she turned away. Then he realized something about all the people around them, something they shared with him and Sofi. "No one has luggage."

"What?" Sofi asked.

"No one here has any luggage or overnight bag or anything

you'd take if you were going somewhere."

It took Sofi a moment before that sunk in. "They're not going on a trip."

"We should leave now." Pax got up from the bench, but that action seemed to cause everyone to turn their attention to him.

Like lions getting ready to jump on their prey they circled the pair. The young man took off his headphones and hoodie. He revealed his well toned torso that was covered with tattoos of arcane symbols. The woman took out a gloved fingerless glove and put it on. The glove itself was long and silky going down her arm and the way the light caught it made symbols appear on it and vanish just as quickly as they appeared. The old man moved closer, his hand clasping a walking stick with a red gem on its handle that glowed ever so slightly as he gripped it.

"Sorry to keep you waiting. I'm glad I wasn't too late for the festivities."

That voice was one that Pax and Sofi had both heard before. They turned to the source of the voice to see the magician from earlier walking towards them without a hint of worry.

A sly smile crept over Bronte's face, "I didn't want to ask for help but weighing the consequence of this whole project I knew that I couldn't risk failing." Bronte spoke in English this time rather than his usual Greek.

The magician walked towards him without a single shred of fear or concern. A wave of power seemed to waver off him and the others as they were all ready to attack. Pax wondered how they had found them. He pushed the thought aside, they would have to figure a way not to be tracked, but that would be worthless if they couldn't get away first. He wished he could still teleport at will but he knew that was not going to happen.

Pax needed some time to try to come up with some sort of plan of escape, "Why? Why go all this trouble for her?"

The magician tilted his head in confusion. "You really don't know, do you? She possesses a unique ability that we need for our plan. She might be the only person in this world with that power."

The woman slapped him on the back of his head, "Bronte, be quiet. I know everyone is getting a little impatient now that we are getting so close to the end, but we have strict orders not to let anyone know anything about our plans." The woman's name was Maeva and her voice was harsh and had a clear French accent to it. The magicians were all speaking English which seemed to be a common language among them.

That was all Pax was expecting and he knew better than to let an opportunity pass him. He took Sofi by the hand and ran as fast as his feet could take him. He pushed past both of the magic users taking them by surprise. The two magic users hesitated only for a second as they watched Pax pull the woman they looked for away from their grasp.

"Stop them!" the French woman yelled. "If they get away we will all end up paying for it. We will all end up like that idiot Redgrove."

That name reminded the group of something terrible if their pained and scared expressions was anything to go by.

The young man with the tattoos reached out for him as the marking on his body started to glow with a strange blue light. Figures that seemed to be made of black flames started to form above him and at his silent command they raced towards the pair. As the figures raced towards them, they took the form of large predatory birds. They let out a terrible caw as their talon like feet reached for the pair. Pax pressed his legs forwards pulling them through the doors before the shadowy figures caught them.

The shadows paused by the door, they were the size of cars and were forced to stop as they couldn't pass through the human sized doors. The pair ran as far and as fast as they could from the train station. As they looked around the streets were all empty. Pax guessed that the magicians had not only nudged everyone away, but they probably found a way to stop the trains. They continued to run with no sign of help or safety around them. Whether it was out of sheer hope of finding salvation or just too afraid of what was chasing them they didn't stop running.

The ground shook and cracked around them. The earth tore from around their feet, leaving only a large hole around them. That was when they noticed the old man with the cane standing at the other end of the hole with a smirk plastered on his face. He was Cezar and old man certainly, but also very powerful when it came to Earth based magic. Age had given him patience unlike his more youthful magicians. The handle on his cane held a small gem that began to glow. He let his index finger tap the gem and the patch of earth that Pax and Sofi stood on shook only to stop again. Pax looked around and he didn't understand it, but the hole around them just kept going down until the only thing he saw around them was black. It was too far for them to try and jump it and he had the feeling that if they fell into it they would fall for a long time. Pax didn't like the bruises he had received earlier that day and he really didn't want to see how many broken bones would feel like. He could tell that Cezar had shaken their patch of Earth as a reminder that he could pull it from beneath them any moment he wanted.

"Great work, old timer." Bronte patted him on the back.

Cezar spoke with a soft Romanian accent, "They won't be going anywhere, unless they can fly."

"We don't need the guy so you can just get rid of him."

Cezar traced the gem with his finger and the ground right beneath Pax began to crumble.

"No!" Sofi yelled and she wrapped her arms around Pax pulling him as close as was possible. "You need me for something and I won't let you do anything to him."

The ground had turned solid beneath his feet again. Sofi had guessed correctly that they wouldn't harm her to kill him. She sighed in relief, believing they were safe.

Maeva cleared her throat and commanded their attention to that small act. "Maybe we can't drop you into a hole with him, but there are other things we can do. They might hurt you, but we only need you alive and it seems that your friend is nothing but trouble for us."

Maeva's glove started to shimmer as she slowly traced

shapes into the air. The air seemed to shimmer at her touch and a strange, almost song like noise filled the air. Sofi forced herself to watch as something started to happen. Sofi could somehow see it if she focused, energy flowing from her hands invisible to most as it started to wrap around Pax's neck. Sofi's eyes widened in horror as she started to see him gasp for breath. Sofi looked at the woman with pleading eyes as if begging her to stop, but Maeva only looked at her with a detached cold look.

Chapter 03: Pax

They say as you die that your life flashes before your eyes. Even a reaper Pax couldn't say for certain until he felt his breath run out. Some people had said that seeing your life flash before your eyes was just a side effect of the brain releasing chemicals trying to survive. Pax didn't understand how that worked but he saw his life or the important parts at the very least.

His first memory was of darkness and then of light. He remembered a gray sand like ground with a huge black tree with spindly branches standing under a pale white sky. On the ground there were countless black pods opening up and black mist pouring out. They all looked the same and Pax knew he looked like that too.

An elegant young woman walked towards the tree. She had long almost impossibly black hair and milky white skin. Her eyes were sharp and amber. She wore a long black gothic dress that wore with an elegance of a queen. Her face broke into a wide and bright smile. Pax wasn't sure how he knew it but he knew she was Death.

She spoke with a gentle but grand voice, "I am pleased to that have you witness the birth of a new generation of reapers."

That was when Pax noticed that around the tree countless forms moved in closer. Among them stood tall Anubis as a small smile spread across his snout as he looked at all the puddles of black mist that were the new reapers.

Every once in a while Death would take some reapers to a tree she had planted in her realm. The tree was called the Tree of Death and like how the Tree of Life connected all those that lived the Tree of Death was connected to all those born in the realm of Death. The reapers were born from the tree and the power of Death and another. Whenever populations got bigger or new ways to die were found new reapers would be born from the tree. Death invited reapers to the birth so that they could help the newborns find their place.

"You are adorable." A man hugged one of the new born reapers.

Pax looked at him and could tell he was different from everyone else there, honestly anyone would say he was different from any one else. That man was the other that gave his power to create the tree and he was known as Life. His eyes were bright and looked like diamonds. His hair was wild and seemed to stand on it end by itself. He had light brown skin and was tall and thin. He wore a pair of well worn brown pants and a simple blue button shirt. He wore a long coat that seemed to be made of multiple colored lights it was almost like the light and color of a rainbow had been shaped into a coat for him. Honestly the impossible coat would be one of the reasons why no one would think he was like anyone else.

"Honey?" Death called to him in a sweet and gentle voice. "Don't scare the newborns."

"Sorry." Life gave the reaper he had been hugging a pat on what he was sure was their head before letting the reaper loose.

The reapers were not of his realm but he still was always there to witness their births. Both he and Death had been together for literally forever and as different as they were they loved one another and were married in their youth. They were as old as the Universe or possible older by some accounts. Despite their age they both looked to be in their mid to late twenties.

Death clapped her hands and spoke to the crowd of older reapers, "You know what you must do."

That was when Pax first spotted her, that was when Pax first saw Valdis. By reaper standards Valdis was still fairly young but she was chosen for this task. Older reapers were selected to help guide the newborns settling into their lives. The young Valdis had a simple black dress on and had long and wild and wavy silver hair. Valdis only looked like a girl about seven years old looking

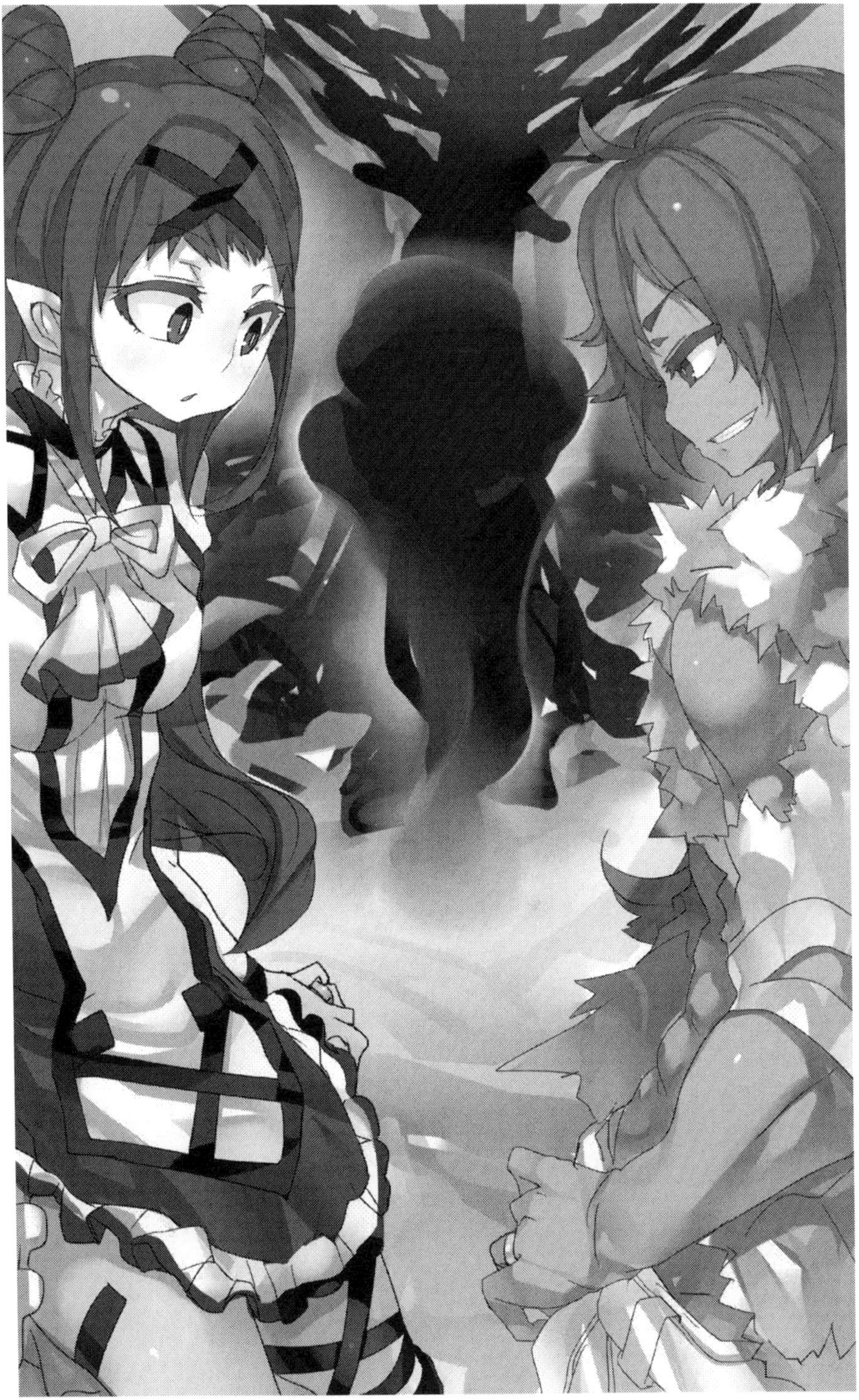

around curiously as any seven year old girl would. It was her first time at the event, if you don't consider her own birth.

"Excuse me." Death tapped Valdis on the shoulder. "If I can make a suggestion, I think that one would be a good fit for you." Death pointed right at Pax.

"Ah." Valdis said trying to hide her nervous tone. "If you think so, My lady."

Death gave a small sigh knowing how all her reapers were so formal with her. "I do think so." Death gave her a small tender smile.

Valdis took a step closer to the small cloud of black. She gave Pax a warm and pleasant smile. "Hello I'm Valdis and I'm going to help you become a reaper."

Death smiled at the new born reaper as she gently caressed him, "I think Pax is the best name for you."

That was how it all started for him. There really wasn't much that Valdis could teach him about being a reaper, most of that came naturally to him. Pax just needed a little help getting control of his abilities just like how baby takes some time to learn how to walk. Still learning such things happens very fast for reapers. What he really needed was help connecting to humans and the true nature of his work.

* * * *

About a month later, during a cold winter, somewhere near a tiny village somewhere in Europe. The actual date happened a long time ago and the name of the village has been lost to time and not even the ancient creatures who watched the village would be able to remember the name.

"It's hard." Valdis said leading along the small black cloud that was Pax. If anyone would see her they would think she would need more clothes as she walked through the snow. "The first time is always hard and that is why you get some help from me and our Lady. The way Trima explained it to me and how Anubis explained to her and who knows who explained it to him is that things have weight. It is like throwing a rock into a river, doing that causes ripples. When a person dies but doesn't naturally move on by themselves that causes ripples in the worlds. It affects reapers like us and we get called to them and we try to help them move on. Today is special day because it's your first day, today our lady is giving us a little extra power. When someone dies like that it doesn't affect the world but it affects time just a little bit, like an echo going backwards so with the extra power we can find them just before they die. I have to warn you that there are other deaths that have this effect, bad deaths, terrible deaths and just days when bad things happen."

Pax stayed silent just hovering behind Valdis and listening to her words.

"Okay, right now your first is just clinging to life. He's still on the side of the living and he can't see us. We are in the Veil, a dimension right next to the living one, just sort of put on top of it, between the Afterlives, Waiting room and our Lady's Realm. Some people can see into this world, people who see ghosts or are special but we only go into the Veil to get the recently dead so normally we shouldn't be seen. I honestly don't think a lot of people would understand what we are anyway."

They stopped on a snow white hill, the only real shape anywhere were a few snow covered trees. The sky was gray and the ground was just covered by snow. Valdis pointed to a small huddled figure on the ground just covered in snow.

Valdis just said, "He's about to die."

Pax looked at the figure to see a small boy who had fallen asleep in the snow.

Valdis continued, "What they don't understand is we do not kill them and even when we know it's about to happen we don't have the right to choose who lives and dies. They die because of a lot of reasons from things like nature and their own choices but we don't do anything to speed it up. You will get a lot of people who will argue and yell and cry but you have to remember we don't pick who lives or who dies, we just help them accept that they have died and help them go where they end up going to."

It sounded important and Pax tried to make sure he'd always remember that.

Valdis said in little more than a whisper, "You can feel it, it's happening."

Before their eyes a small a confused boy appeared next to his body. The soul had left his body when he died but it had not left the world. The dead soul had taken on the form of his body in life and become a spirit but not yet a ghost.

Valdis told him, "He's in the Veil with us he's a little confused so he hasn't noticed us yet. We help them move on because if they don't and stay here lingering in between the worlds they will start popping up in the real world. Being outside the world like that starts to wear away at them and make them crazy and dangerous. The spirit will fall apart and turn into a ghost that moves away from the Veil and into the world of the living. So help him accept that he is dead and let his life go so he can move on." Valdis small hand patted Pax on what she thought was his head. "Remember how I taught you to change your appearance. Its time to do it, make yourself look like something he can accept and will help him."

Pax had been told by a lot about people and when his first test arrived he had no real answer come to mind.

"Trust your instincts." Valdis told him gently.

He never knew why he choose that form but Pax turned from that black cloud into a black and white copy of that boy. The only thing with color were his bright blue eyes that stood in contrast to the boys own brown eyes.

The boy looked at the reaper with surprised and shuddered a little taking a step back. In a small tone he asked, "Who are you? Are you one of the spirits mama told me where hiding the forest waiting to take me away?"

Valdis walked over to them having a hard time trying to figure out how to answer that questioned when it wasn't too far from the truth. Valdis wondered silently why a reaper who specialized helping children move on such as Alma wasn't called to help this boy move on. Valdis had the feeling that this wasn't going to be easy

"Well, you died and I'm here to lead you to the other side. The not being alive side." Pax tried to explain it to him.

There was a moment of silence. Pax had to repeat it to the young boy several times and explain it.

After several minutes the boy explained what he had been doing, "I wanted to play outside but mama told me it was too cold. I didn't listen to her and put on my winter clothing and ran outside. It was cold but I had fun and explored. I wandered away and I started to get tired. I thought I had fallen asleep."

It was a painless death if anything, he just got cold and numb and fell asleep. Valdis was glad for the small mercies the universe had granted the boy. Even as a reaper she didn't like to think of the deaths of those so young. To her experiencing so much death didn't make it any less painful she was just got used to that pain.

The boy insisted on seeing his parents. Now that he was dead he didn't feel cold or anything and raced to his home. The reapers followed close behind. They arrived at a small home nestled in the middle of a small village. The boy found that he could walk through walls but he soon forgot about that as he found his mother crying. The village had all gone searching for the boy when he vanished and people were scared when they didn't find him. The boy tried to call out to his parents and begged for his mother to stop crying but they didn't hear him. This went on for days.

That is the making of a ghost. When a spirit who doesn't move on because they don't want to or just manage to escape their reaper stays on the world. Being separated from everything and everyone they knew slowly seeps away their humanity. Valdis thought that maybe that was the lesson Pax was sent to learn. Sometimes reapers would fail and things like ghosts would appear. The idea was to get the spirit to accept their own death and move on but for the most part reapers weren't able to force them to move on.

Valdis whispered to her fellow reaper, "Talk to him. Try to get him to move on."

"How?" Pax wondered.

"I don't know, this is for you to decide. Use what you know."

Pax walked over to the boy who sat in the corner as he watched his mother cry unable to stop her from crying. "I think its time for you to move on."

"Why does she cry?" The boy asked innocently.

"She is sad."

"Is it because I died?"

"Yes, I think so…" Pax looked at him. "I think it's because you are still here."

"I don't want to go, I don't want to leave her."

"She is your mother and you will always be her son and with that comes a connection. It's called love."

"That's good, isn't? I love my mama and she loves me."

"Yes, but from what I have been told about it…" Pax paused trying to think of the right words, the world was so new to him but he been told much about people and their emotions and their hearts. "Love can also hurt. She can feel you here and she can't let you go until you let go and move on."

"Why can't I stay with her?" The boy looked up at him with eyes filled with tears.

Valdis spoke up walking towards them, "The truth is you can. You are not stuck in a body and you don't need to eat or sleep and we can't make you go."

"You have that same tone that mama uses when she tries to make me do something." The Boy told Valdis.

"I can see it in your eyes…. you are so young and not as strong soul. Spirits who stay behind lose themselves. If you stay you will start crying out to them and all the grief will cling to them, to your mama and papa. You will start to forget them and just want to be around them without understanding why. You will be nothing but an echo and you will still be here years and years after they are gone."

The boy paused, "I don't remember my name. I forgot it yesterday and I haven't been able to remember it."

The room was silent except for the weeping woman.

The boy stood up and walked to his mother and his hand just touched her face and the woman shuddered at the touch that she didn't really feel. The boy pulled away suddenly. No one could say how long he knew what had to be done, it might have been something he understood the moment he died or it could have been only a second ago.

"I'm ready to go." The boy said softly. "What do I have to do?"

"Just take his hand." Valdis told the boy.

Pax reached out his hand to the boy, that was all that was needed. They boy took the reaper's hand and the moment they touched a light engulfed the boy. A sense of serenity came over him as the light covered him completely. He turned back at his mother one last time and said in a whisper, "Good bye, I love you."

The boy and the light vanished with a wisp. The mother suddenly stopped crying and said weakly, "Good bye."

The woman to the day she died never knew why she said that at that moment she just felt that she had to. She was sad for a long time after that but at that moment she started to feel that her son was at peace.

"Our lady will take it from here." Valdis explained. "She will take care of him and take him where he needs to be." Valdis gave the young reaper a reassuring smile. "You did well, he's in a better place."

As Pax watched these memories play out before him he realized the boy had told him his name but after so many years he too had forgotten it. Then Pax realized something else, that his current appearance was what the boy would have looked like if he had grown up. He never once thought about it and he didn't do it intentionally but in some way he always remembered the boy.

* * * *

Another memory started to play before his mind's eye. Several years had passed and became decades and then became centuries. It was an age of revolution, the time of the French Revolution and the Reign of Terror. Pax had found himself in France with hundreds of other reapers. During times of disasters, of wars, of chaos, of many deaths reapers were summoned to help with the many people who had died. At these times the usual type of people they specialized did not make any difference they just had to move as many people as they could.

Pax sat at the edge of a stone building watching the streets below. He liked France for the most part, this was a day he didn't like it. Years later he would remember how romanticized the events would become in plays and movies and he would always scoff at them. He couldn't understand how people who were so afraid of death and dying would go into mobs and drag people to their own deaths and revel in it.

Pax now looked to be in his twenties and wore simple black outfit. His hair was messy and his eyes were tired, this was the first break he had in days. He had just helped a woman move on after she fell and was trampled by a mob that didn't even notice her.

"Out of the way!" The familiar voice of Valdis pushed him down onto the roof.

"What?" Pax asked.

Valdis now looked like the teenager she looked like in the modern day. Her silvery hair was in a medium length pony tail. She had on a long black wool coat over her simple and ankle length black and red dress. Valdis was on top of using her body to push him onto the roof just as a large scaly and thin leg swept past them. Pax looked over to see a giant green spider about the size of five men. It was sickly green in color with bright red eyes and red marking over its body. It smelled like rotten flesh and the drool that seeped out of its jaw smelled ever worse.

The spider was a member of a species called many things, a Soul Eater, a Devourer, Spirit Demon, and a Death Eater. They were creatures that sometimes ate the flesh of the dead but enjoyed eating the souls of the newly dead. Like their cousins the Ghouls they feed off the dead and were born in graveyards but they took animal forms unlike ghouls who mostly looked like undead humans. A place like France during the Reign of Terror would have been an all you could eat buffet for it and it looked like it was trying to eat all it could as it had grown so big. It was a small miracle that people hadn't seen it, it would have caused a panic if they had. The roof under the Death Eater cracked and withered with each step it took.
     "Valdis, have some sense this is no time to flirt with the boy." Another reaper walked until she was standing between them and the Death Eater.
     Pax couldn't help but yell out, "Nila!"
     The reaper before them was a tall woman with light brown skin. She wore white pants, thick black boots, a gray button shirt and she wore a long blue military coat. Her hair was a short wild brown mess. Past her half circle glasses her lime green eyes glimmered.. Her hands gripped a pair of black and silver flintlock pistols.
     The steps of another could be heard. A man with gray skin and a black robe just walked care free to the side of the creature. His long silvery hair fell over his eyes. He held a silver and very long scythe decorated with engraved skull all over its handle.
     He chuckled, "Do I have a story for you." He swung the scythe at the spider forcing it to pull away.
     "Morton?" Pax questioned the new arrival.
     "All this death caused by the people drew this big fellow here. It started to get a taste for spirits along with rotten meat." Morton swung his scythe again letting his robe sway around him. "Then we found out this thing has been starting to attack reapers. Tried to take a bite out of poor Foster."
     Nila spoke up shooting at the legs at of the spider only for

it to avoid the attacks. "We found out it spotted you and Celeste at the bakery that caught on fire. Celeste got called away to Italy so she was safe. So, we had to find you and who better to find you than the reaper who can always find you?"

"Be quiet." Valdis jumped off Pax and onto her feet. She pulled out a long silver sword that she had hidden in her coat. It was a Xiphos sword, bearing a silver leaf-shaped blade with a golden handle wrapped in black leather. It was longer than most swords of its type which gave her a longer reach. It was thin and light, but it felt strong in her hand. The sword was old, well maintained, but old, showing its years with small scratches which covered the weapon. Despite this, the sword gleamed as it was new, ready to take on yet another opponent.

Ignoring the anger in Valdis' voice Morton decided to continue, "Lady Death sent us to deal with that little Death Eater but Valdis was more than eager to help when she found out you were its next target. I wonder why?"

Valdis pouted at the other two reapers. Suddenly a huge thud as a black figure fell from the sky right behind the spider.

Pax jumped to his feet and stood straight, "Marik!"

A tall figure all in black stood behind the spider. It was a tall medieval knight whose armor was all black and didn't show any sign of exposed skin or any sort of weak spot. Through the metal grate on the helmet two glowing fiery orbs that were his eyes glowed green. He held out a large black sword. Marik was the reaper of warriors, warriors that would only agree to move on after they were beaten in battle. Some of the fights that reaper had against spirits were beyond intense. Other reapers respected him if they didn't fear getting on his bad side.

His voice boomed and hung in the air, "I see you've managed to corner the beast. We wondered if you'd manage to do anything."

"We?" Pax asked him.

The air seemed to grow colder at the moment. Suddenly something flew from the lower floors of the building onto the roof.

The Death Eater seemed to shuddered at the large wavering black figure. Floating above them was a cloaked figure holding a black and silver scythe.

"Grim? The Grim Reaper." Pax gulped as he saw that very reaper.

The Grim Reaper was not only a powerful reaper but one well known and feared even by the other reapers. He was quick and clinical and had no problems about showing himself to humans especially when he had many people to collect. Grim held a scythe, a tool and weapon made by Death and given to him to wield as he saw fit.

The spider didn't last much against the team reapers most who were battle ready. Valdis stayed in front of Pax to protect him while the other reapers attacked. A flurry of energy was released and with the various physical attacks cut through the spider, cutting it into ribbons. The ribbons were then reduced to goo and ash. The attack were powerful enough to destroy the beast in moments and causing the whole section of the city to shake and most of that was just one attack from Grim. People had no idea what happened but left area thinking it was some sort of riot and left with a feeling of dread. Those reapers had weapons given to them by Death, Grim's being the far more powerful one, and with those weapons they easily over powered the monster that threatened the dead, people and other reapers.

Still Pax remembered how Valdis came running for him the moment she thought he was in danger. You know you have a real friend when they actually run towards something that could eat them just to save you.

And things weren't always heart breaking lessons or fighting something huge that wanted to eat him. Sometimes they even had fun.

* * * *

Pax could still remember a night over a hundred years later, sometime after the first world war.

There was an alchemist who had found a way to stop aging and managed to never get sick. Normally such a person would not be visited by a reaper but the Alchemist did get in an accident with an elephant. Though that story by itself could fill a book we're not going to get into it at all. It's an entertaining story but it can cause nightmares to some people, I know I'd have nightmares if I ever actually had any sort of dreams.

What Pax had started to remember was the following day after the accident. The Alchemist had managed to make his way to his apartment above a bar he had owned. The Alchemist had made an elixir to hold off his own death by aging and he was using to keep his body from stopping even after an accident which should have killed him. The Alchemist was somewhere between life and death and a reaper was sent to get him to move on. That reaper was not Pax but one known as Anlon. Anlon was a reaper that dealt with challenges, he would challenge the soul and if they won the soul would agree to move on and if they didn't these reapers could do all sorts of things including revive them if needed.

Anlon had confronted the Alchemist agreed and being the one challenged he was the one to pick the challenge. The Alchemist picked a drinking contest using some a barrel of a wine so strong that some gods thought it was too strong. They each took one drink at a time deciding whoever lasted the longest would win. That went on for a few hours. It had started late at night and just before the sun started to rise on the small bar in Spain it was still going strong.

Other reapers had come to see the contest and they started to have less strong drinks and a party had started. If the Alchemist were to win and continue the bar he was going to make a small fortune. Valdis had dragged Pax to the contest that had spiraled into a reaper party. By this time they had both settled into their current look more or less.

Anyway, Valdis had probably had too many drinks and wasn't thinking straight.

Valdis had gotten a little tipsy that even as she sat down

next to Pax she needed to lean on him just to avoid falling.

"There is something I want to tell you." Valdis manage to say clearly.

"Okay." Pax said not sure what to make of it.

"I have known you a very very long time."

"It does feel like forever sometimes."

"You are grumpy, you are grumpy pants man."

"Yeah, you've told me that before."

"Why do you have to be so grumpy?" Valdis shook her hand spilling some of her drink as she spoke.

Pax quickly took the glass away from her to stop her from spilling more on him. "Well, you've had too much. Let's get you home so you can sleep."

"No, no, no and ……" Valdis forgot the next word she was going to say.

"No?" Pax guessed her next word.

Valdis spoke slowly and her words were stretched out. "Yes, that's it. I want to tell you something. It just seems stupid that I haven't said it before."

"What you trying to tell me?"

"You are one of my oldest friends."

"Well, most reapers are old friends, not the ones that are jerks but-"

"You are special." Valdis just ignored whatever he was saying. "You are special to me. I really can't think of how my life would be without you."

"That's very sweet, it's a little said that you've got to be a little drunk to say that." Pax couldn't help but get a few lines in. Pax gave a small sigh, "Yeah, I think the same about you."

"That's the thing I don't think you understand what I am trying to say. You are very stupid and very stupid about these things." Valdis was drunk but she wasn't wrong about this. Valdis pulled him close and looked him deep in the eyes. "Me and you, that's what I'm talking about. You mean a lot to me. More than I can really put into words in a way that can make sense. The only way I can say it is that I...." Valdis took a breath as her face started to turn red. "I love..."

"You love what?" Pax still had no idea what Valdis was trying to tell him. He waited for a moment for her to continue. That was when he realized her eyes had closed, in the middle of the conversation she had fallen asleep and her head tumbled into his chest. The drinks that the Alchemist had were strong enough that it had the same effect on reapers as normal liquor had on humans. Pax took off his suit jacket and placed it on Valdis.

Valdis snored lightly as Pax picked her up into his arms. Pax chuckled at the reaper in his arms as they teleported away. The contest continued into the morning and eventually Anlon won and when they both woke up the Alchemist was happy to go to the other side just to get rid of his headache.

Pax took care of her that night and found her somewhere to sleep. He took care off her until she was up. Valdis woke up amongst the flowers of a small island of Maui as the Sun rose above her. Valdis quickly found Pax's jacket covering her as she slept, she pulled it close when she noticed Pax sitting a few feet away.

Pax greeted her with a kind smile, "Good morning."

Valdis jolted up, "Morning!" Her face turned bright red and then she forced herself to toss his jacket at him.

"How are you feeling?"

"I'm okay." Valdis didn't make eye contact with him.

"Good, I thought it was a good idea to keep an eye on you until you got up."

"Well, thanks for that."

"No problem." Pax scratched his head. "So, last night before you ....fell asleep you wanted to tell me something."

"What?" Valdis said as she started to remember the events.

"You love something?" Pax said with an innocent smile. "What do you love? You said you wanted to tell me."

"Oh, I don't know. I must have forgotten."

"Oh well." Pax sighed with a shrug.

Valdis looked at him through the corner of her eye and muttered. "Idiot."

I personally don't disagree with her statement. Pax really didn't know what Valdis loved despite it being obvious to a painful degree.

If Pax took away anything from the moment was to enjoy life. He had great and fun friends and despite his overly serious nature. He always found himself enjoying his life when he got to spend some time with a dear friend, Valdis.

* * * *

Wonders also played out in his mind. He had lived a very long time and he had seen so many things. There was one that stuck out in his head, one special moment that happened decades later. It was a book store in Chicago during the 1980s and sounds almost the exact opposite of wondrous but that moment was. A woman had died, in fact she was the owner of the book store and while trying to fix a high up shelf she slipped off the ladder she had been on and a copy of War and Peace, in the original Russian, fell right on her. The fall wasn't that big but the way she landed and how the book landed on her head caused a quick death for the woman. Pax had been called to help the woman when she died and showed up but there was no spirit.

"This is a false alarm."

"Huh?" Pax questioned the voice and he turned around to find Death. "My Lady?"

Death looked the same as when he was first born except she had updated her clothes for the era. Death was now wearing a black business with large box like shoulder pads. "Hello Pax."

"What are you doing here? She can't be someone that you come for, right?"

With a flash of light Life appeared next to her, his rainbow like coat waved and shimmered with all it's colors. Under his coat he wore a pair of black slacks and a rainbow colored tied-dyed shirt. Life picked up a book, "She is very special or was or will be.

These things get a little confusing when tenses get involved." Life tucked the book into his pocket.

"Are you stealing the book?" Death asked him.

"Deatz, I don't think she's going to care." Life stood besides the dead woman.

"Deatz?" Pax questioned the name.

"It's a name he made up for me a long time ago. People close to me have called me that for years because of him."

Pax notice the fact that despite that being a complaint she almost sounded happy at the fact. Then he noticed that she too took a position beside the dead woman. They each moved a hand over the woman until their hands joined. Slowly a small white orb of air like light appeared on their hands. That small orb could be described in a million ways, a small storm of light and energy, a song given form, a story given shape, a million feelings all gathered together but when it came down to it was a soul. A soul that hadn't lingered in pain or grief or anything to turn into a spirit but simply was. Pax had seen souls like that before, usually he saw them when ghost or s spirt started to move on.

The room was empty except for the three of them and that was sort of shame because Pax thought it was beautiful. Reapers saw souls but really only got glimpses of it as they moved on, ghosts and spirits and things were souls wrapped in energy as they projected themselves so seeing a soul like this was something. The soul is the core of every living thing something of theirs that survives through even death. The light of the soul stretched out filling the room with its light, now none of them nor the soul were visible in any wave of light that normal people could see but if someone was there they would feel it.

Pax could just tell things about the woman from the light of her soul. The woman had known heart ache and pain but she was smart and loved a story. She was a woman that loved music and color and enjoyed life. She was a warm woman who had a gift to make people smile even when they were sad. She knew love and knew what it was like to be loved in return. She was mother and if she had time for one last thought she would have worried about her son.

Then it just vanished and the room seemed to grow colder because of its was no longer there.

"It's done." Death, who I will call Deatz from here on, said out loud.

"A cat." Life tilted his head.

"What?" Pax said confused. "What just happened?"

Deatz simply told him, "Reincarnation."

"That can't be right. Don't people who get reincarnated skip the call to reapers, they just sort of die and pop up where they go to just like other people when they die and head to you to go to their after life."

"Normally yes but there are exceptions to every rule." Deatz admitted to him. "Her soul has been preordained to reincarnate for a long time."

"She is getting reborn as cat." Life told him. "Somewhere in Tokyo as a little gray kitten. I hope she will have a happy life for as long as that one last."

"Preordained?" Pax asked.

"It means to have been decided or determine beforehand." Life defined it for him.

"Yes, I know what it means. So you decided to-"

"We didn't decide anything." Deatz told him. "It was decided by a higher power."

"Higher than you two?" Pax couldn't really wrap his mind around that idea. "Who Destiny?" Pax said jokingly.

"My little brother does like to play his games to see how things play out but no." Deatz confessed. "I meant a much higher power."

Life jumped behind her and pointed upwards to the ceiling almost like his arm and finger were trying to pierce the heavens. Deatz was more subtle and just pointed up with her index finger.

"You mean....?" Pax stared upwards for a moment.

There were certain figures or ideas in culture including

45

someone that stood above all and created all. Pax certainly had thought about it since many people had asked him. Truth be told he wasn't really all that sure if there was a God or anything like that. He certainly knew there were powers and forces beyond his understanding. He couldn't say he had faith in any sort of power that just seemed to human a thing for a reaper. He knew of Death and Life and just trying to imagine something grander than them seemed too much for him. The very idea of something like that made him feel so very small and that scared him just a little. Pax tried to focus on the here and now. He turned to what was before him.

    The whole scene before him with Life being the model of display of energy while Deatz was much more reserved and subtle became a comedy in contrasts. Pax couldn't help but smile at the sight. It was silly but Life seemed perfectly suited for the silly but Deatz had only seemed more serious but she gave Life a quiet and bright smile. Pax saw something there, something everyone could see, that connection the pair shared a connection that could only be called love. Most people would say that Pax was old but those creatures were far older than him, so old he couldn't wrap his mind around that length of time. The truly amazing thing to him was that after all that time those two still adored one another. That smile and that look they shared was all the proof he needed for that fact.

    "Pax?" Deatz turned to the reaper with a small voice. "You'll have excuse us it's our date night."

    Life wrapped his arms around her and kissed her cheek. Pax couldn't help but wonder how many times they had kissed but every kiss seemed to still bring forth that joy for both of them. They both vanished into nothingness.

    That day Pax had seen many wonders, a saw a beautiful soul, he witnessed a reincarnation and he saw a love that had literally lasted ages. He certainly couldn't make of what to think. Pax decided right then and there never to admit it but one day he would love to find someone that could make him feel as they made each other feel. Someone who he could share just a smile and he would be filled with delight. Pax was more of romantic than he could ever want to admit. He had lived a very long time, longer than most people could imagine. He had seen a lot of things through that time. Still he wasn't tired of life, that day showed him there were still mysteries he didn't have answer to, there were joys that he had yet to experience and there were wonders yet to be seen. There were things he still wanted to do and see.

* * * *

He had seen many things but his memories seemed to turn back to Valdis. It was decades after Chicago. Only a few years ago, they had a day off, the people they normally collected just weren't dying for that day, and Valdis insisted on doing something together. Valdis took him to France and they spent the day together. They saw some art and did some very tourist-y things. Then they had crepes. Valdis really insisted on the crepes, she loved her snacks.

Anyway, Valdis had gone to get seconds leaving Pax at a table. That was when things went odd, a magician managed to stun him and drag him away before his fellow reaper returned. Pax woke up with a headache in a dark underground room.

The room was dark and from the odd shapes he could see covered in shadows it was some sort of storage room. One light bulb hung over his head giving the room what little it had. Pax saw a figure near the door speaking into a cell phone. Since the figure didn't bother to pay attention to him Pax decided to leave. Normally a reaper could move to another location with little more effort than a thought but this time it failed to work. Looking around the reaper spotted a large book on a nearby table with an old illustration of a skeleton like figure in a black robe. Looking down on the ground Pax found a chalk circle around him with arcane symbols drawn around the circle's edge. The circle and the symbols had the right shape and form to hold the energies that made him, to tether him in place.

"Oh, a bidding circle." Pax groaned out.

"You're awake." The figure spoke with a soft and almost

innocent voice putting away the phone. "I was wondering how long that spell would keep you knocked out. I had never used a spell on a reaper before."

"Don't worry about it." Pax looked him up and down. "Reapers aren't easily hurt."

The figure almost glided above the ground towards him. The figure moved into the light to reveal a smiling boyish face. The young man before him had shinning green eyes and neat hair the color of dying leaves. He certainly looked young but Pax had lived long enough to know that things weren't always what they seemed.

"So, what are you?" Pax asked him.

His smile didn't fade even a little. "Isn't that usually what people ask you?"

"I think we both know what I am. What are you? A magician? A wizard? A necromancer? I don't really care for titles but I do try to be polite enough call you by whatever you want to be called."

"You can just call me Redgrove."

Pax tried to figure him out but he was someone hard to figure, his accent seemed to be an odd mix of many accents from all over Europe. Redgrove wore an old plain brown suit which didn't reveal anything about him. Pax wasn't even sure if Redgrove was his real name since he knew people who used magic often hid their names.

Pax asked him, "You dragged me here for a reason, do you mind telling me what that reason is? What do you plan to do with me?"

Redgrove's smile grew a little. "How could I pass up a chance to capture a reaper? I was walking down the street and I saw you for what you really are. I've studied reapers but I've always thought you stayed hidden behind a veil. You normally stay hidden to all but those who have died."

"It was my day off and I was talked into walking amongst the living. You still haven't answered my question, what do you plan to do with me?"

"Knowledge is power and with a reaper I could certainly learn many secrets of death and gain some power over it."

"It looks like you already have a lot of information on that." Pax pointed to the book.

"Not true at all, the information on reapers is rare and most of it very old. I thought it was time to refresh everything. Magic is the art of manipulating the energies of life and you are creatures that claim the heart of life."

"The soul?"

"The soul is said to be the greatest source of energy anyone can hold. The soul is the keeper of the heart and the spark of life, imagine what I could do if I knew how to claim it like you. My cabal has plans and that sort of knowledge could benefit us greatly."

Pax is a very easy going most of the time but for once in a long time his face harden. "I cannot say I'm a very good reaper but I'm not one bad enough to let someone harm souls. What you want to do with your own soul is your own business but you don't have claim over any other soul." Pax's resolve was clear in his dark stare and strong tone.

"Oh, that was impressive. I think that gave me chills. Are planning to play the hero?"

"I'm not a hero, I'm just smarter than people think I am."

Redgrove sighed, "What is that supposed to mean?"

"You have me in a bidding circle so I know I can't escape it until someone breaks the circle, so I'll just wait."

"Wait until I die of old age?" Redgrove scoffed at the idea. "That could take some time. If you intend on doing something to me with your powers you should know your powers will not work in that circle."

"I told you that I'm not playing the hero. I'm the guy that makes mistakes. Maybe in the end reapers are reflections of who we collect. Maybe it's simply because we spend so much time with those types of people or maybe that's part of our design. I made a mistake and let myself get caught. If this gets out the other reapers will tease me for years to come." Pax rolled his eyes annoyed at the very thought. "Anubis will never stop lecturing me."

"How is any of this supposed to stop me from forcing you into telling me what I need to know? Is any of that supposed to stop me from just studying your body to find out what I want to know?"

"It is really simple: you don't have a true purpose for power. I've seen your kind before, kings and emperors who gather power thinking it will keep them safe or make them happy, but it doesn't. Most of the time it brings danger and pain. The only people that gather power and don't have it turned on them are those that use it to help others and don't hurt others to get it. You crave knowledge and power for your own benefit but don't think of anyone else. In the end that is what will stop you."

"What is that supposed to mean?" Redgrove's smile started to fade as he started to get annoyed.

The loud sound of metal being cut apart was heard. The large metal door to the room fell inwards in two pieces. Standing in the doorway was a petite figure holding a sword that glinted a silvery light. Her eyes shone in the darkness like a cat's predatory glare.

"What took you so long?" Pax greeted Valdis.

"It wasn't easy to find you." Valdis said with a smile.

"Another reaper!" Redgrove said his voice filled with shock.

"A very angry reaper at that. I go back to our table to find my friend missing and someone making sure I can't trace him. So I think I earned the right to be angry."

"I have this entire room filled with wards to keep reapers out and make sure no reaper could find anything in the room." Redgrove told her.

"True, so when I searched to find nothing I thought if someone took him they might be hiding him. So, I looked for a room I couldn't find and this is the only room in the entire city I couldn't see into. It was just a big black empty space. It was just like looking for wind to find the invisible air. Then the wards to keep me out stopped working when you don't have a door."

"You found us because you couldn't find us." Redgrove deadpanned, he took a sword handle from his pocket and with a flick of his wrist a sword formed. "Well, I have a sword too."

Valdis simply smiled and gave a half shrug. She spoke with a smooth Spanish accent, "You killed my father. Prepare to die."

"I did no such thing!" Redgrove shot back.

"Sorry." Valdis giggled as her voice returned to normal. "Both of us had swords and I just got carried away." Valdis raised her free hand over her head and leveled the sword with the other.

"Why does a reaper have a sword?" Redgrove couldn't help but ask as he readied his weapon. "I always thought a scythe was the tool of the reaper."

"No, just the reaper who carries one loves the attention." Valdis smiled showing no fear of the weapon he pointed at her. "I got this sword from a hero who fell in battle after slaying a terrible monster. With his final battle won he went into death and left me the sword. I try to use this sword only for the best reasons and I can't think of many better than saving a friend."

Pax realized something, "Wait, does that make me the damsel in distress?"

Valdis laughed, "Only as the old styled ones, the modern ones would have tried to escape on their own."

"I knew you'd find me." Pax tried to explain it to her. "I was stalling until you showed up."

"I don't mind playing the rescuing hero." Valdis continued to giggled as she jumped forwards and the swords crossed."I'll save you in a moment just let me slay this bad warlock." Valdis gave him a playful wink.

Redgrove was quickly pushed into playing defense as Valdis slashed away at him at a speed impossible to humans. Redgrove tried to move out of the way but only managed to block the flurry of attacks. Whenever their swords hit they sent sparks out in every direction. Redgrove slowly moved towards his left, slowly guiding the reaper around in a circle. The idea was to get her to fall into a pattern and eventually step into the circle to trap her too.

"Do you really think I'm going to fall for that?" Valdis stopped moving before her foot moved into the chalk circle. "I'm not going to step into it even if I'm a little distracted."

"What?"

"I only let you move me into place so I could free him." Instead of pointing the sword at Redgrove she slashed the tip at the chalk circle. Just brushing away some of the chalk was enough, the circle was broken and like a cracked cup the small break let what was inside out.

Pax took a step out of the circle and stared down the magic user. "Now let's talk about your plan for using me to get souls and power."

"We can't let you go and do that." Valdis smiled peacefully. "Our duties as reapers include protecting souls."

Redgrove took a step back knowing that fighting one reaper unprepared would be hard but fighting two would not end well. His phone started to ring and that seemed to give him more reasons to be scared. "Oh, no, they know. I'm-"

The room rumbled as a bolt of lighting struck Redgrove out of nowhere filling the room with light. When it passed there was nothing left but a small crater and some ash. It confused the reapers as they didn't sense his soul waiting to be claimed.

"Was that the boss?" Valdis asked putting her sword in its sheath that she hid under her coat.

"I don't think so." Pax told her. "He said he had plans and I guess his cabal thought he might talk and yanked him away. Whatever, he's out of my hair." Pax smiled glad that everything was over and had ended well.

It was odd for him to smile. He found that most of his smiles for the better part of the last few centuries were the result of something Valdis did. He didn't have a single doubt in his mind that Valdis was someone very special to him, someone very important to him. He really didn't know how to describe that relationship. Valdis would always come running to him should he ever nee help. When Anubis was furious with his work during the Boxer Rebellion Valdis was the first person to stand up for him. When he flirted with a Valkyrie and was tossed into a mountain Valdis was there to pick him up and cheer him up. When he upset the Grim Reaper...Valdis didn't actually do anything she was scared of Grim too but she did help Pax put himself back together afterwards. Valdis was always there when he needed her. Pax regretted that he never said thank you to her. Pax regretted that he didn't say anything like good bye.

* * * *

Pax wondered what would happen next. Would he die and meet Death and she would hug him and tell him he had a good life? He really did think he had a good life. He had great friends that sometimes just made him angry but that he cared about. Pax wondered if he would linger on the world and a reaper would show up for him. Maybe it would be Anubis, or Grim, or Thanatos. He wondered if they would scold him or maybe they have some kind words. He hoped Valdis would be there. Part of him didn't want Valdis there, he was certain that she would cry for him. He didn't want to see her cry. Maybe he wouldn't get a spirit that lingered, he was a reaper and even in a human like body he was not truly human. Still, he wanted to see Valdis again even if just to say good bye or tell her she important she was to him.

He could feel his lungs crave air. The world around him started to fade away and blackness took its place. As he could feel his life come to an end he gave one last look to his past and to the faces of the people he cared about and were important to him. To a colorful man and a black and white woman, a wild woman dressed in blue, a black shadow, a woman dressed in black with a flower in her hair, to a black knight with greens orbs for eyes, to a silvery gray man, to a woman in white, and so many other reapers he had known. He thought of the young woman with green eyes, Sofi, and how he failed to protect her. He thought of silver haired Valdis one last time, he thought of her smile and how she seemed to be one of the few people who could always cheer him up. Valdis was also the person who always saved him but this time he knew she wouldn't be there.

He felt weak, he felt weaker than he had ever felt before. Then he started to feel nothing and he could only see black, he couldn't even see his memories anymore.

He felt a soft hand caress his face. It was cold and gentle and in that short instant he knew whose hand it was. He had to know, she had caressed him like that before on the very day he was born.

Chapter 04: Light and Shadows

A smart man once said that time is relative, I wasn't talking about myself but thank you for thinking I'm smart, anyway he was right. For Pax the time he saw the highlights of his life it seemed like a few hours. As Sofi watched in horror as Pax was being strangled it was only a few seconds. She saw the flow of magic wrapping around his neck cutting him off his air. For a moment in sheer panic she stared in shock. She tried to shake him and she tried to grab the magical energy that wrapped around him and tried to rip it off. Sofi found despite the fact that her power allowed her to see what was invisible to most she still couldn't affect it. As Pax's body started to go limp tears started to stream from her eyes.

"Please!" Sofi screamed. "I'll do whatever you want! I'll go with you just please let him go!"

Maeva held up the glove and gave Sofi cold stare. Maeva looked over to Bronte but he only shook his head.

Maeva's face didn't so much as flinch and remained emotionless, "I have to agree, he's been a lot of trouble and you really have nowhere to run to."

Maeva wasn't a very kind person, she was in fact a very direct and often times violent woman. If she saw something she needed to get done and she had to hurt people to do it she wouldn't hesitate to resort to violence. Who is to say why she was so violent? She had great promise and power since at an early age. She knew what it was like over power others easily and after a while with that kind of power you sort lose connection to other people. After a while some people who focus on power can just not see people as being anything equal to them. So, if she had to kill Pax to guarantee her mission she would do it without worry, especially since she knew what prize awaited them at the end.

Honestly she could really get a lot of help out of a good

therapist, and so could Bronte for that matter.

It was a moment that Sofi knew would burn into her mind for the rest of her life. Pax had only tried to help her not even asking for anything in return and now he was giving up everything for nothing and she could not do a thing.

Then something soft an gentle cut through air, a simple playful piano tune. It was cheerful and light and full of spirit, which would not have been what Pax would choose for the last thing he'd hear.

A tune that really didn't fit the mood of the moment at all and something so ill fitting caught everyone's attention. They all turned to see giant floor piano set at a near by park for a street performance. It was a large set of piano keys that were rolled out and actually functioned like a regular piano with an addition of speakers. The performer had to jump around on the keys to play a song so the performer basically was a dancer and musician at the same time. A hat that people were to drop money into was left by the side of the instrument but along with the piano it was left behind when the spell convinced every person away. The person on the keys with her back to them, she looked like a small woman with long silvery pig tails. She danced on the keys performing a rendition of the song Chopsticks.

It was Valdis jumping up and down the keys to get the right notes and suddenly vanishing to the other side to hit the other keys. Her long black coat swaying with each note and her long silvery hair bouncing up and down with each and every jump. With the final note done she jumped off the keys and with a quick spin turned around holding her right arm up to add a little flair to her landing.

The world was quiet again. Valdis blinked as she finally saw what was happening. Her eyes went wide as she saw her friend in danger. She only showed up to check up on her friend and teleported near where she sensed him. The first thing she saw was the piano and thought it would be a fun way to get his attention but was unaware what was happening.

Now there are countless of reactions to seeing something like that and Valdis picked a drastic one. Valdis vanished only to show up next the French magician with her sword drawn. That action caught everyone by surprise but not as much as when Valdis cut off her gloved hand with her sword. Maeva screamed as the hand was sliced off and she saw nothing but a white hot blinding pain as she fell over. The silver blade was sprinkled with blood as the magician screamed and lost all control over the spell she had been doing.

A small sound escaped Pax's throat as the invisible rope vanished. Sofi caught Pax as he started to fall, she had a brief moment of hope that was quickly forgotten when she felt how cold his body was. There was a killer intent in Valdis' eyes as she slashed away at the magicians. The ones that weren't in pain decided to attack the reaper at once hoping to put her down quick. Bronte chanted a spell and lighting gathered in his palm, that man with the tattoos created an eagle made of black flames and launched it at her, Ceazar pointed his cane at her and red energy exploded out of it. The air grew hot and seemed to shudder at the release of energy as the attacks raced towards the reapers. A shadow almost mist like black energy wrapped itself around the blade as she swung it at the spells fired at her. With that one swipe the spells were torn to ribbons and the air erupted backwards as the energy exploded. The magicians were tossed backwards while the reaper focused the blast towards them with her sword.

The magicians who had all the control only a moment ago found the tables turned. They stared in horror at the childlike reaper brandishing a sword at them.

The old man shook as barely managed to ask, "What are you?"

Valdis spoke through gritted teeth, "A reaper and a very angry one at that."

She swung her sword at the ground and the streets exploded towards the magicians as a huge cut formed in the ground. The black energy quickly vanished off the sword as she gave them a cold stare. Valdis quickly placed the sword back into its sheath beneath her coat. Valdis decided her attention was needed elsewhere and she grabbed Pax. Valdis didn't even notice Sofi holding on when she teleported them away.

Bronte held his hand to the large gash on his forehead. He stared at the destruction around them and took a second to look at the now unconscious woman who was missing a hand. The others had their own share of wounds.

The magician with tattoos was known as Calvin, no one called that as no one seemed to think that name suited him and his usual stoic and silent nature. Now Calvin stood and stared in horror at the damage before him. In a panic he spoke for the first time that week, "That was a reaper. They know! We have to tell him! If they know why we want the girl they won't hesitate to stop us! We are too close to be stopped now!"

The others looked around the damage that one reaper had managed to do in seconds and they all paled at the idea what an army of those monsters would do to them.

****

Sofi gasped as the world had been replaced by black and then turned into an empty hotel room. It wasn't the one she had been earlier this one looked even more expensive. Valdis took them to the hotel room on the top floor, one so expensive that it was rarely ever used. It's actually more of a suite than a room.

Valdis quickly put Pax on the very soft bed. Valdis had been present on many battlefield and disaster sites over the many centuries and had seen many people try and resuscitate people but she lacked any experience of trying it herself. Valdis jumped on Pax and pressed her palms onto his chest trying to restart his breathing.

"Come on! Come on!" Valdis begged as she pressed his chest up and down. Tears started to pour out of her eyes as she started to lose hope. She was desperate and at this point she decided to try it. She took a deep breath.

Life in any form can often be brought down to energy.

What Valdis had planned was basically something like jump starting a car with a battery. Valdis braced herself and she leaned in and pressed her lips to his. It was certainly not how she had imagined their first kiss. The air in the room started to shutter around them. Valdis was slowly transferring some of her own energies trying to use it to heal and keep his living connection to his soul. Valdis had never done anything like that, as far as she knew no one had tried this and it was just an idea. If she didn't do this correctly she could destroy any chance of saving him and possibly damage her own body but she decided to try.

There were bruises on Pax's neck and that was just the external damage that could be seen. Sofi gasped as she started to see the bruises heal. It was slowly like watching water drop drip down a window. The action was as simple as taking a breath and just as important. Pax's face became flushed as without thinking about he started to kiss her back. Valdis' lip quivered a second as she kissed him and her body felt weak, that wasn't totally because of the kiss she had just given up a lot of her own energy.

Kisses are interesting things. In fairy tales it has often been the case that true love's kiss could lift any terrible curse. There are stories of the kiss of death, which mostly sounds like bad thing. The kiss of life is also a thing, which does have a better reputation. I suppose it depends on your preferences.

Okay, I've just been told that neither of those kisses has anything to do with either of the people called Life and Death. So, that is my mistake and sorry for the confusion.

Back to what I was saying, there is a certain something about kisses. Your first kiss is something that you always remember. They are rarely good, they are clumsy and you don't know what you are doing but they are special. The first kiss with someone you care about could be something special that you carry with you every moment of your life, something you think about in you worst time which helps you smile and carry on. A kiss like that can make you feel strong and weak at the same time. Anyway you put it I would certainly say a good kiss is like magic.

Pax opened his eyes and realized who he was kissing and he would always remember the kiss and the shock he felt in that instance.

Pax pulled away realizing he was kissing Valdis and said, "Mommy!"

"Mommy?" Valdis said more than a little annoyed that was his first word after their kiss.

For any guys reading this, don't say mommy right after you kiss a girl. Actually that goes for girls too even if you are not kissing another girl, generally people don't like being referred by the person they kissed by the name they called their parent when they were two. That whole thing just gotten awkward very quickly.

"Valdis!" Pax shouted that out of pure reaction.

"Yes, I'm not your mom." Valdis reacted in kind.

He quickly grabbed the smaller reaper and hugged her tight. "I saw her. I saw Death. It was only for a moment but I saw her." His voice wasn't powerful or confident, it was just low and quiet.

Valdis hugged Pax right back, "You're okay now. I managed to fix you, drag you back from the edge."

"That is dangerous and Anubis is going to yell at you, give you a whole lesson about doing such dangerous things and if I had gone all the way...."

"Shush." Valdis smiled hugging him a little tighter. "I don't care, he can yell at me all he wants the important thing is that you are safe."

"So, you have a girlfriend?" Sofi decided that this was the best moment to speak up. With the whole nearly crossing over because of serious injury both reapers had forgotten the young woman that was in the middle of all this. I honestly don't blame them a lot of things had happened.

"I'm not his girlfriend." Valdis gulped and managed to say that.

"She's not my girlfriend." Pax quickly said.

Valdis turned to Pax and gave him a half glare, "You

answered that a little fast."

"What you're not my girlfriend, you are a friend that is a girl."

Valdis let out a huff, "I did just drag you from the edge of the veil."

"Yeah, you are more than a just a friend. You are probably the best friend I could ever have and thank you. I mean it, thank you for not only saving me but always being there to save me."

Valdis nervously gulped, that might not have been the exact thing that was hopping to hear from him but that certainly not something she hated to hear. Valdis truly did care about him and she really did think of him as her friend even if she thought of him as a little more too.

"Are you going to get off him?" Sofi broke the tender moment by reminding them that Valdis was still on top of him.

There was a yelp that Sofi couldn't tell if it came from Valdis or Pax or maybe both but a moment later Valdis have leapt away off him with a bright red face.

"Huh." Valdis cleared her throat. "Pax, rest a little and you need to get something to eat. Human bodies need food to get more energy. I'll have to get Anubis to look you over and make sure you are okay."

Valdis quickly moved towards a small kitchen that the hotel had in the room. She looked through the draws and refrigerator to see if there was anything to eat.

"I didn't get your name." Sofi walked up to her a sort of edge in her voice.

"Valdis." The reaper replied rather quickly. "And what's your name?"

"Sofi." Sofi said stand offish like manner.

You could say many thing when meeting someone but some of the things that are conveyed through tone and body movement. Their tone made it seem like a fight was about to start. Both women were tense, rightly so, since it had been such a hectic day. They both stared at each other in silence.

Sofi decided to break the silence, "Aren't you a little young for him?"

Valdis glared back at her, "I am actually older than him."

"You have to be kidding me."

"No, reapers can make themselves look like anything we want and look any age we want."

"And you just chose to look like a little girl?"

"I look like a teenaged girl that is not a little girl."

"No, you look like a little girl and the hair doesn't help."

"What's wrong with my hair?"

"You mean the school girl pigtails? Or the silver that you don't see outside of grandmothers?"

Valdis fought the urge to pull out her sword again.

"I pick my appearance very carefully."

"Why would you choose to look like that?"

"I choose to look like this for the people I have to collect." Valdis said softly and seriously. "Each and every reaper collects one type of person. Each reaper helps one type of people move on and let go of the life that they have lost. My group is the ones you'd call heroes. Most heroes end up dying in battle, or trying to save someone in danger. It's not all glorious like people think. Very few get to live a long time and die surrounded by loved ones." Valdis spoke with a serious tone. "Heroes are often driven to their limits and are left broken. They don't always show it but the path of the hero takes a toll on them. I often show up to find them in bad shape. People in that state like being around children because it reminds them of innocents and makes them feel that the world is not all bad. I think this form reminds them of what they died to save, so children could have lives and play in the sunshine. I think looking like this makes it easier for them to accept everything. So do not make fun of something I choose to be to help those who need help and those who should have the end of their journey be a smooth and an easy one."

Valdis liked to play games, she liked sweets and junk food, she liked to make jokes and some would just call her silly but don't

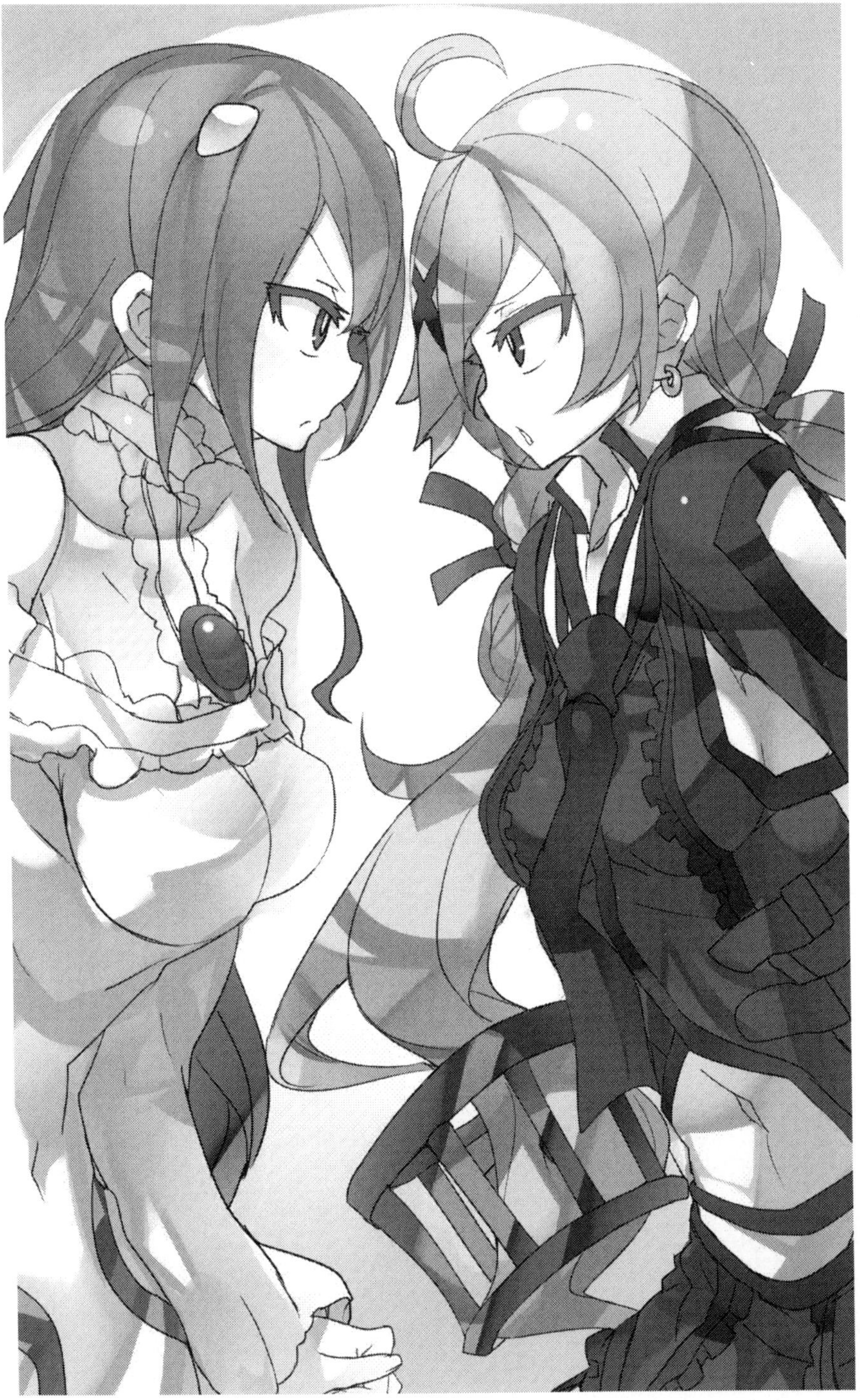

ever think she doesn't take her job seriously. Valdis doesn't think her job is easy or even consider it a noble duty for her but she does know that it needs to be done and will do everything she can do to do it right. She has been on horrible battlefield with a sole person having to fight over impossible odds to make sure someone is safe. If she was called there it didn't usually have a happy ending but most of the time the heroes managed to save people, someone they cared about, the world, or even just one person and that seemed to make their sacrifice worth while. Valdis couldn't imagine not doing everything she could to make it easier for them to move on.

Sofi was actually surprised to the reaction she got from the reaper. It might have been simply because Valdis looked like a child but Sofi hadn't expect a mature and deep response from her.

"What does any of that matter?" Valdis tried to shake the whole talk off. "Why do you care? Why are you here with him? What happened?"

Those were a lot of questions and most of them were pretty valid questions to ask.

"It's hard to explain." Sofi tried to be honest. "I'm not even really sure about it. I have this power or ability." Sofi tried to start off slow. "It lets me kinda see things, to know things. The second I saw Pax I saw the same thing I see in you. You look like a person but you're not, it's something smoky and black."

That got the reaper's attention, that was how reapers looked like when they were first born before they picked their appearance unless Pax told her about it very few people on the planet could even know that. "What?"

"I was in a circus and then this wizard guy showed up, the one with that cloak."

"Magician." Valdis corrected her. "Wizards are born with power and that guy was drawing energy from the world and object and wizards and use their own body to directly draw power from the nature or the world or some sort of god."

"Whatever, that is not important. He started chasing me all across Europe. Then I ran into Pax and the magician tried to fry us with a bolt of lighting. Pax helped me and tried to get me away from the other guy and he brought friends and attacked us at the train station. We started to run and they caught us and then just started to choke him with magic. Then you showed up! You tossed them aside like nothing and we were suddenly here. I still don't know who you are or why you decided to make out with him!"

Yelling doesn't help and it certainly didn't help that she was clearly jealous.

Valdis let her lower lip stick out in an almost adorable pout, "My name is Valdis I am a friend of Pax and reaper of heroes. I helped him on his early days being a reaper. I have known him since the days before the countries of Europe looked anything like they do now."

They're both pretty old.

"I'm Sofi......" Sofi tried to come up with anything that could sound half as impressive or as intimidating as what Valdis had just said. "He saved me today." Sofi didn't come up with a single good idea. "So, you just happened to show up when he was in trouble?"

"Yes." Valdis admitted. "I promised I'd show up and check in on him right before he was sent here to live as a human. The first break I had I came here and looked for him." Valdis hesitated to think of what she could have found if she was even a second later.

"And you were so relieved that you kissed him?"

"I saved his life." Valdis explained as her cheeks turned a slight pink. "We are both reapers even if he's sort of human right now. We are creatures made of energies of death and well...." Valdis looked away. "I sort of gave him some of my energy to help keep him going. It helped heal him and just get his heart going again."

"And you had to kiss him to do that?"

"I had to get that power into him quickly or it wouldn't work. That was the only way I could do it in time. The second fastest way I could think of was cutting something open and that would just make more work."

It wasn't a lie but it was the entire truth. It was the best way it transfer some of her energies to him but she knew deep down she wanted a kiss too. She cared about Pax for a long time and she had tried to tell him how she felt but things had gotten in the way, most of the time it was actually her nerves. Pax was her best friend and if she said anything and he didn't return her feelings that she could lose that friendship. Valdis didn't know how she would cope without his friendship at the very least. It didn't help that the other reapers would often tease her about her affections and even hint about her crush to him right in front of him. It also didn't help that Pax could be dense about these things.

Just thinking about it was adding to her frustration, she sighed and ran her fingers through her hair.

"It's…. it's just-" Valdis started. "It's just I love him." Valdis let those words out like they were a breath. Valdis waited so long just to say those words out loud and after what she had just been through she felt like she just had to say them or she would never get to say them at all. "I've loved him for so long and I've never found the courage to tell him and I saw him today and ….."

Sofi watched the reaper as she let her words trail off. She knew the pain of losing someone, she had lost both her parents and had spent many sleepless nights thinking of all the things she wanted to tell them and all the things they never got to tell her. She had dreams about what life would have been if they lived to raise her. Sofi could only imagine that things were the same for reapers, that if they lost someone they'd always wonder what could have been and be pained by knowing they never did.

In a way that was how she lead life, Sofi acted and tried to live in the moment. For the most part just going with what felt right worked for her. She knew this was likely living with her ability, she saw things and felt things from others and that became her nature like when people took warning seeing the color red. If she felt something was dangerous it probably was.Though she had only known Pax for a short amount of time she knew he was special to her and that she truly cared about him.

Love is a tricky thing. Love is not something you can just sit down and give a perfect definition for. Some people will say they fell in love at first sight and they have been in love since then. Some people will tell you that there was always something there and love grew out of it. Some people will say that after knowing someone for sometime loved bloomed. I can't really say that any of them is a less valid form of love. The conflict boils down to a girl who fell in loves over time and has been in love for a long and a girl whose fallen very quickly into the thing called love. They looked each other in the eyes and they understood the situation.

"You too?" Valdis spat out the words.

"Me too what?" Sofi knew exactly what Valdis meant but just didn't want to say it out loud.

"Don't pretend you don't know." Valdis was tired and she was not willing to pretend that they both didn't know.

Sofi sighed, "Yeah, I don't know how to say it but there is something special about him."

"I've known that for a very long time." Valdis said almost like she was staking her claim.

"So, why haven't you said anything?" Sofi replied with the simple comment.

"You can't understand, you just can't, you can't understand knowing someone so long that you just can't imagine a day without seeing them and then saying something that could wreck everything you've known. You can't understand the fear of loosing that all."

"What are you talking about?" Pax called out to them.

Both Valdis and Sofi froze with the realization that Pax was literally just a few feet away and had heard their whole conversation. It was a hotel, a nice one and spacious, but hotels don't usually have that many walls between the sleeping area and kitchens.

Pax continued to talk, "Who are you talking about? I know it's a hectic day and at some point I think I hit my head but I have no idea what you're talking about."

Their jaws dropped, Valdis knew he could be like this but it still surprised her. Pax was very good at being able to sense what emotions people were going through but for one reason or another he could never seem to understand when someone liked him. Many reapers pointed that fact out when they brought up his less than impressive love life. Valdis suspected that might have been a reason why the few romantic relationships he had never lasted, and that was something she feared when she thought about admitting her feelings to him.

Valdis let out a long sighed shook her head, "Go to the rest room and splash some water on your face."

"That's probably a good idea." Pax got up from the bed and went into the bathroom.

The moment he left the room both Sofi and Valdis sighed in relief. Valdis was not in the mood to go through that today.

"Did he really not-?" Sofi asked the reaper.

"Yeah, he does that. Some of the other reapers have made a game out of it, they give him hints that I like him to see if he can figure it out and just watch me squirm." Valdis turned away from her and looked into the refrigerator looking for something to eat. "So, he got hurt because of you."

Sofi felt a dark lump in her throat when she said those words, she would love to say that it wasn't her fault but in the end he was only there because he wanted to help. Pax was still a stranger but he decided to help and had decided to save her and she loved that about him. "Yes, he was trying to help me and those guys didn't want him to try it again." Sofi spoke in little more than a whisper.

There was a thud as Valdis let her head slam on the refrigerator. "He's not a warrior. There are a lot of reapers that can fight but he is not one of them. He doesn't have to deal with insane spirits or the dangerous things that run in the dark. He really shouldn't be apart of this."

There are those that thin reapers are just reflections of the type of people they collect. If Valdis was ever anything she certainly was hero to Pax but did that mean she could save others too? Could she make the hard choices when the time came to make them? Valdis had many discussion about that with Pax, she assumed that he always felt like a mistake himself even if he never mentioned it. She never knew how to argue it, the reapers that collected the souls of people who were as good as monsters were as scary as monsters to even other reapers. The reapers of warriors were warriors themselves but she didn't know if it meant she was a hero and she didn't think Pax was nothing more than someone due a mistake.

Valdis took a breath and focused the conversation on a new topic. "Let me rest and I will get you somewhere safe. I don't know what you are or why these magicians want you for but I think I can help. Reapers can move anywhere we want, well more or less."

"Yes, I got the idea of that when you did it."

"Yeah, we're still in Vienna and we should move. There are places around the world that magic is strong like Stonehenge or Kyoto or Uluru or really most of England or Southern California."

"Southern California?" Sofi was confused to why that place was added to the list.

"Yeah, you'd be surprise. The important thing about it is that if there is a strong place for magic and there are also weak places for magic. Possibly the greatest place were magic is weak or just not working is Lebanon in Kansas."

"What?" Sofi was more confused about that than the Southern California comment.

"I know it sounds strange but most magical folks won't even go there unless they have to. Lebanon is the center of the continental United States and all the natural energies and the energies that people move around are not there. It's a magical dead zone so much so even gods are weak there."

"Does magic really work like that? Like a cell phone in a bad area?"

"Sometimes, magic is just about energy. Wizards and witches are normal people who just happen to be connect to the natural energies of the world, or other worlds, or spirits or gods. They can draw the energy and with the right words, chants, rhythmic sounds, symbols, rites movements can shape the energy and use it to shape the world. Then there are people who learn to tune themselves with these forces or even use magical items to help get the energy. Items that have special meaning or belief behind them if not just raw power."

So looked at the reaper before her with wonder, "And in Kansas it won't work?"

"Well, nowhere near as it normally does. If they can track you with magic they won't be able to track you in that city. The energy lines are so weak in that city that even normal people who have nothing to do with magic don't flock there, it just sort of feels a little wrong to them."

"Will I be all right?"

"Sure, it doesn't hurt anyone even people with powers. At worst it might make your power a little weaker if it runs on magic."

"I guess that might not be bad, it I might not mind not knowing when someone is lying to me." Sofi ran her fingers through her hair. "Will you be able to take us there? I mean, won't it affect you too?"

"No, magic is something that runs on life energy but reapers are creature of death so our powers don't run on that. The ones that I know that learned magic have to draw the power to run it from nature and things like that."

"Are you sure you can take me there?"

"Yes, I'm sure. I've never been there because the population there is so small that there isn't a lot of need for reapers to come but I have heard of it from some reapers that have been there."

"You know I was excited about learning that magic and things like reapers were real." Sofi says a little sheepishly. "I mean, I always thought I was strange, and the only thing like me but now

I know I'm not. It's a shame that I have to go to a magical-less place now."

Valdis tried to work out her best smile for her, "Its better to be safe and alive and knowing about magic than being dead. Trust me, I've met a lot of people who've stumbled into the world of magic and the incredible but they often regret it. The thing about having life with all those wonders is that if you accept that as your life you can't walk away from it. You get all the wonders but you get all the dangers too. You get one choice, one chance to walk away and you might want to take this one."

Valdis was sincere about the warning, every reaper knew that those who dealt with the supernatural often ended meeting a reaper faster than others. Many people met their end encountering some dangerous creature or some powerful entity. Actually, Anubis held a class about that subject once a year. It wasn't a popular class but it was only for one day so some of the more dedicated reapers tended to go to it.

Anyway, a moment later the door to the bathroom opened up and Pax walked out.

Pax let out a sigh, "That has to be my least favorite thing about these experience 'Human life' vacations." Pax grumbled to himself before he looked at the other two. "Valdis, you have that look."

"What look?" Valdis raised an eye brow at that comment.

"Your 'I have a plan and its perfect' look."

"I don't have that kind of look."

"I've known you for centuries and I think I can say without any fear of being wrong that you have that look and that is it."

Valdis now pouting, "Well, I know what to do. You've heard of Lebanon? You know, the place in America where magic goes all plop."

Pax stared at her, "....Yes."

"If you don't know it's okay. Well, since magic won't work so well there then I don't think magicians will be able to use any magic to track her. If she avoids getting on the news or anything like that she will be safe until this all passes."

Pax thought about it for a second, "That is actually pretty good."

"That's perfect and you know it." Valdis poked Pax with her index finger.

Pax smirked at her, "Yeah, okay, I will give you that."

Sofi watched the two reapers playfully tease one another. Sofi wondered if there were more things like them, things that were so different yet so human. Part of her screamed for her to stay in this wonderful world of possibilities. Another part of her told her to hide and go to where she would be safe. And a large part of her was silent not sure how to take it all.

"Are all reapers like you two?" Sofi asked.

They paused for a moment, looked at her and said together, "No."

"You should see Anubis." Pax told her, he mused for a second, "Once we get you settled maybe I can get him to see you. He's probably the oldest reaper I know and besides being a bit a task master he is very smart. He might actually be able to figure out what your powers are."

"That's not bad." Valdis told him amazed. "He does like puzzles, he might actually enjoy helping you. At least he might be able to help you learn to use them, he's one of the best teachers I've ever had."

Sofi smiled, for one moment she had hoped that she would be safe and still see into this world that was just in her reach.

Hope is a light that help you get through the darkness. The important thing about light is to remember that they might make you feel safe but you should never forget the darkness is there waiting.

* * * *

And something else was waiting in the darkness. A woman sat on cushion in a darkroom somewhere far away. She wore nothing but black and a single white candle sat before her, the only light in the room. She had long black hair and her breathing was so slow that it almost looked like she was dead. Some people might have said she was meditating but really it was something more. Her name was Tula but some people called her the Lady of Shadows for a very good reason.

Her eyes suddenly opened up to reveal pitch black orbs.

"I found her." Tula's voice was like a wisp of a fire being put out.

Bronte moved towards her, "You found them?"

After the attack they had to retreat and got help, especially the one that had lost a hand. He was forced to get help and the magician before him scared him a little.

Tula held out a small stone with a blood stain in her palm, "Your spell was enough for me to track her and with my powers I can do much more."

Tula had mastered shadows, she could travel through them and listen and hear through them. She had become apart of the shadows so much that all shadows to her were just extensions of her body. She was able to listen to their whole conversation from the shadows beneath the bed.

"You are in trouble. They plan to take her to a magical dead zone and if the reapers are protecting her then a fight there will mean you losing everything."

"Reapers? As in more than one?"

"Yes, a man and woman who looks like a girl. They are both weak at the moment but that won't last. You know everything that we have been working for depends on that girl. This is the one chance you have to make it all right. Attack with everything you have."

Bronte took a deep breath, "Do or die, then? How can I refuse such an invitation?"

Chapter 05: Into the Dark

Valdis hummed to herself, "Just give me another minute and we should be ready to go. I think we need to make a quick stop first."

"Oh, please tell me it's not another one of your snack runs." Pax bemoaned.

"It's not just another snack run!" Valdis shouted at him. "We are going to get pizza at in New York. There is this place that makes great pizza, it's called Original Ray's...... Or maybe Authentic Ray's....Spectacular Ray's? It's one of those places."

"Are you going to try to make this whole things trip go try all those places?"

"What? Is it wrong to get a snack to fuel me up?"

"No, except you don't actually need to eat."

"No maybe I'm making sure you get something to eat."

"Some greasy piece of bread?"

"Good pizza doesn't have to be greasy it also has rich tomatoes sauces and fresh meats and vegetables. So it can be a tasty snack or meal along with being a good source of nutrients."

"Say what you will but you will never get me to believe any of that."

"Not that this isn't a wonderful conversation." Sofi spoke up. "I still don't get something." Sofi figured since they didn't seem ready to leave that she might as well find out a little more about them. "You said magic wouldn't work in this place you're taking me to. You also said you could take me there because your powers aren't magic. So here is my question: how do you do that whole teleporting thing if not magic? I'm pretty sure it's breaking some laws of science."

"Because we're not magic." Valdis started to explain. "It's hard to explain it to you. People tend to have this idea of binaries, that something is what it is because it isn't something else. Black is not white and white isn't black, you guys forget about grays. Magic is one side of a coin and science is the other. Both magic and science are ways people not only understand but connect to the universe and control it."

Sofi nodded at the lecture the reaper was giving as if she understood though she wasn't sure she did. "I think I get what you're saying."

"But magic and science have their rules and work with energies and forms."

"So, far I think I follow but that still doesn't answer my question."

"Like I said that there are grays. Magic and science as each one side but reapers and the being that created us and gave us power fall on the edge of the coin. The rules are a little different for those who fall in the middle ground. That area is for creatures have connections to the Universe older and stronger than most can imagine and use energies drawn universe itself. Creatures and entities like our boss, Death, can call upon power right from the Universe and control aspects of the Universe to the point that they can bend, twist and warp reality. I heard that some people who can get a hold of this comic power can do that too but they have to get raw power that is hard to find these days, power that hasn't been around the universe since the dawn of time." Valdis paused to let the knowledge sink in. "The reapers are more like echoes of a fraction of Death's power. We draw power from Death so we aren't anywhere near as powerful. We are each given a touch of that power that we draw from Death's realm, so its not nearly as strong as the power that Death can draw from the Universe. Its like second hand power. We can't do anything like change the world at a whim but we have all the power we need to do our duties as reapers." Valdis crossed her arms and gave a proud nod what she held to as her culture. "We can change our forms, teleport around the world and even into the nearby dimensions and realms, release some of the energies to attack if we need to and a few other tricks."

Sofi remembered when she watched Valdis attack the magicians and saw how she let lose an attack on them. Sofi wasn't surprised that Valdis wasn't able to move them at the moment is she released that much energy it would take some time to replenish it.

"What is your favorite type of pizza?" Valdis turned and asked Sofi.

Sofi was a little surprised that Valdis was so eager to continue the pizza talk.

The peace of the moment was quickly shattered, first there was a rumble that shook the room before finally the roof exploded. A red hot force broke the roof apart sending pieces flying everywhere most burn up in the air and turned to ash. It was pretty random action but one that sent the trio apart. The reapers were tossed to one side and Sofi was blown to the opposite side of the room. As random as that seemed it was actually planned. Like lighting Bronte appeared in a flash of light and grabbed Sofi.

"Quickly wrap them in the chains!" Bronte barked the orders as the other magicians appeared in similar displays of lights.

The reapers were both stunned by the explosion and the other magicians quickly placed chains on them, not just any chains but ones with engraved symbols on them. Sofi's ears were ringing because of the explosion but she started to see the desired effect on the reapers. She saw something black and cloudy beneath their human forms, their essence that she had seen this whole time, and the chains seemed to make the clouds react to the symbols. The clouds seemed to recoil from them and pull in close.

The roof was little more than giant and gapping hole whose edges were red embers quickly eating away at the walls. The damage around the room was mostly limited to the roof and some dust, the explosion was contain since they wanted to make sure that Sofi escaped unscathed. For the most part it worked leaving only a few cuts and bruises on her skin. Sofi noticed similar injuries on the reapers and she even noticed the wounds on Valdis starting to heal before her eyes but they stopped the moment the chains were placed onto her.

Maybe she was still stunned by the explosion but Sofi only watched and the magicians whispered words and placed their palms on the reapers heads. With a little bit of magic they manage to put the reapers to sleep. Sofi was surprised to see such powerful people just taken out of action like it was nothing. That was more than a little surprising so much so that she didn't notice Bronte place his palm on her head and whisper a short spell.

And with that her world went dark.

The world is filled with great wonder but also of things that are dangerous and should be feared.

Hours passed before the spell started to wear off. In the time that the trio was asleep forces moved into place and these people were the ones to move those forces. Years of planning were coming into play all because of one person.

* * * *

Valdis woke up on something soft. The reaper cracked open her eyes to find herself somewhere dark. It looked like some sort of tunnel with brown bricks all around. Every few steps there hung a light bulb from the ceiling lighting the path a little bit but it still left the tunnel pretty dark. Valdis stretched out trying to clear her mind when she realized what she was using as a pillow. Valdis flinched back when she realized she had been using a sleeping Pax's chest as her pillow. She moved back as far as she could but didn't get far when she realized she reached a wall. To make things more complicated for her she realized that she actually hadn't reached a wall but still couldn't move any more. She pressed her hand to find it pressing against an invisible wall, ripples formed in the air whenever she touched the wall.

Valid jumped to her feet and punched at the air as hard as she could and rippled spread all around them.

"Oh no, no, no, no." Valdis started to panic.

Below their feet a circle about three meters around had been painted. Though that itself didn't sound like anything to worry about that circle was made of magical symbols that captured reapers.

Reapers couldn't even touch the circle once in it and trying to touch it form the other side would likely get them tangled up in it. Valdis reached under her coat for her sword, a swipe with the sword would be enough to scratch off some of the paint and free them. Then she froze in place when she realized that the sword wasn't under her coat. Naturally she looked around for it and quickly and found it on a nearby table. The magicians had seen her use the sword and were quick to take it off her just to be safe. On the table were a few magical relics and tools along with a very old spell book opened to a page with a picture of a grim looking reaper with a black cloak.

In the time known as the Black Plague the Grim Reaper became well known appearing in cities where countless were dead of dying not even bothering to hide behind the veil. He collected souls by dozens and those who lived and caught a glimpse of him never forgot. As the disease spread over Europe the story of the Grim Reaper spread and even some magicians spotted him. It was because of that magicians learned to take action, they had plenty of chances to try to stop him hopping to stop deaths not realizing Grim didn't cause those deaths but collected the result of them. In the end the magician's attempts didn't stop death but they certainly learned more about Death and the reapers. They found out which binding spells would work, what symbols would bind a reaper to a spot, how to hide from reapers and even how to stun them. The Grim Reaper was powerful enough that none of the new and unpracticed magic could hold him too long but after time they were more refined. Most of that magic was forgotten when the plague died down and people realized it was at best a stalling tactic. Valdis silently cursed Grim for showing off so much. She took out her frustration by punching the ground below her creating more ripples in the small space between her fist and the circle. The force of her punch was great creating a lot of ripples that spread the force of her punch out.

The ripple were enough to wake up Pax. "Ah!" Pax jolted up startled and looked right at Valdis. He asked, "What happened?"

"We got knocked out and trapped in a reaper's trap." Valdis punched the invisible wall to show how effective it was. "We are good and trapped." Valdis collapsed onto the floor. "I'm sorry."

"For what?" Pax quickly replied.

"I don't know, for everything. For sending you to Vienna, to where you got nearly strangled to death, for getting you into trouble for not just sending you farther away when I teleported us."

Pax looked at her sadly and smacked her head, "Don't be stupid, how is any of this your fault? You didn't know I'd run into Sofi and get involved with magicians willing to kill. You can't be blamed for anything and you shouldn't blame yourself. I'm not your responsibility." Pax let out a sigh, "You know what I was thinking about when I was dying? I was thinking about you. I was thinking about how whenever I was in trouble you'd save me and how I wished you'd be there to save me again."

"I kinda was."

"Yes, you were and you always save me."

"You're making it sound like a bad thing."

"It's not but sometimes I think you do too much for me, like you think I can't get by without you. I have to stand on my own sometimes. You are my best friend and I am thankful for everything you have done for me and for once let me save you."

Pax stood up tall and smiled at Valdis with a smile with such confidence that it made her heart soar. Then Pax turned around and simply stepped out of the circle.

"What?" Valdis asked more than confused.

Pax just smiled at her, "I'm not a reaper. I have the mind and soul of a reaper but my body is human right now, or at least mostly. I don't have any of our power just the knowledge of language that I was born with thats still in my mind. Thats the only difference between me any other person so that trap won't work on me." Pax wasn't lying that the symbols didn't stop him but it certainly made him uneasy and made him feel like his insides were shaking.

Valdis stared at him with a blank look, "You just had to walk out! Why did you give me that whole speech about saving you and everything? Were you trying to look like some sort of hero?"

Pax looked around and found the sword quickly on the table next to the book and took out the silver blade from its sheath. "No, you know me, I talk a lot when I'm cornered." Pax raised the blade and slashed at the painted symbols on the floor until the circle was broken.

"Oh, I just think you can't face your feelings and can only express yourself when you can't run away." Valdis still annoyed walked out of the now broken circle.

Pax handed her back her sword. "I don't run away from emotions. What would make you think that? You are not my therapist."

Valdis took a good look at her sword before she placed back under her coat before she turned to him with an annoyed look, "I've known you a very long time and I think if you were more in touch with your feelings you'd be less grumpy Mister Gloomy Pants."

"I'm not gloomy." Pax quickly shot back. "What you call gloomy is just thoughtful and introspective."

"Yeah right, you are as deep as my belly button."

"Why are we even arguing about this?"

"Because I like your smile and I would like to see it more and maybe you'd do that if you were more open."

"I'm more open to you than I am to anyone else." Pax sounded almost offended by her comment.

Valid looked at him a small blush forming on her cheeks.

A slow clapping filled the tunnel and a harsh voice with a French accent spoke, "You two are having such a sweet moment. Are you lovers? Is that why you react the way you did?"

The sound of her foot steps coming down the tunnel were

steady and confident almost like the beating of a heart.
"You." Valdis let it slip when she saw who it was.
"Yes, me." She spoke rather calmly.
Valdis stared at the woman, the very woman she had slice her hand off.
"Wait, why do you have two hands?" Valdis made a keen observation.
Maeva raised a hand and it was black. To be more exact it was a black stone with runes engrained in silver that was carved into the shape of a hand. What gave Valdis a small scare was that it was attached to her arm in place of her real hand and the fingers moved just like a real hand. "You have a magical prosthetic hand?"
"A gift from my superior, he said it was to make up for the one I lost in the line of duty." Maeva stopped under the light.
Her skin looked sickly pale, probably from the blood she lost with her hand. Her eyes made Valdis uneasy, she had seen those eyes before in the eyes of killers and monsters whose minds were only filled with the idea of causing pain. That is someone you want to avoid even if you're not the one that gets their attention.
The air was still and even a blind person could tell something bad was coming Valdis' way. Valdis didn't think of herself as a fighter but she drew her sword once more.
Valdis wasn't looking for a fight and that wasn't why she carried the sword. Yet she knew it was a weapon and she knew better than most what a weapon did and was made to do. The moment she accepted the sword she knew she had to learn to use it properly. Other reapers knew how to use swords and over the centuries she had trained with them to learn to use the sword. Valdis had practiced with the sword often enough but the problem is even after centuries she had rarely used the sword in a real fight. In a sparring match you fight but don't try to really hurt one another and you practice in ideal circumstances so it's almost nothing like a real fight. Valdis also had no idea what this magician was going to do and that made her nervous. It was one thing to surprise attack the magicians and keep them off guard but this time

Maeva knew what was going on.

Magicians powers tended to twist the world and bend it to its side, if it was possible they might just be able to do it. So Valdis was sure they might have a way to hurt and even kill her. Reapers could live a very long time but only the stupid ones fooled themselves into thinking they were truly immortal.

Maeva smiled a smile that made Valdis more uneasy than a young soldier in the middle of a war. "You must be so old and I cannot help but to wonder if you are wise too. I wonder how long you will survive."

Maeva rammed her black fist into the ground and suddenly the floor erupted, the explosion was focused and like a stream the force move right at Valdis launching her back down the tunnel and into the shadows.

Maeva walked calmly down the tunnel, Pax moved in front of her shaking in fear. Maeva didn't even focus on him but on the spot that Valdis had been launched to, "Move aside."

Maeva didn't wait for him to react but slapped him with her new hand, and that slap was enough to launch him to the side and imbed him into the tunnel wall. The French woman continued to walk into the tunnel. "Bronte, take care of him."

Pax heard steps as she walked away and then heard a crackling sound. He turned his head to see the magician in his cloak with his hand out stretched and sparks of electricity popping off. The light from the sparks illuminated his face just enough for Pax to see his smile.

* * * *

In another area of the tunnels, in a large wide room Sofi started to wake up. The first thing she saw was the old brick floor and the poorly lit room. She couldn't make out many figures around the large room but she saw two large metal circles on the walls. That was when she realized that she was mounted onto a metal cross detailed with symbols. Her body was tied onto the cross with some rather strong rope that wouldn't let her go.

It took her a moment to realize that someone was standing in front of her just in the shadows.

The man before her spoke in an English accent, "Are you awake? I apologize of my people were little rough in bringing you here."

"Why do you have me tied up?" Sofi screamed at him.

With a calm tone he said, "Use your inside voice, Miss Héderváry."

That got Sofi's attention, "How do you know my last name? How do you even know anything about me?"

"We know a lot about you. We know about your father David a Hungarian painter of minor note and your mother Maria an Austrian musician with some talent from what I have been told. Her parents thought David dragged her down and stole her away, but they were young and in love and decided to travel around and take in the world. They only had one daughter, yourself, that they traveled with never settling down in one area for too long. Then one night there was a wet road and then came the accident that claimed their lives. You survived and were taking in by a friend of the family in a circus. You've lead a quiet life doing various jobs in the circus until my man showed up. The most fascinating thing about you is a certain ability that you have."

"How do you know about any of that?" Sofi started to get worried.

"I did research over a very long time."

"Who are you?"

"My apologies, I haven't introduced myself. You can call me Talbot."

"What only one name?"

"I'm sorry but names have power and I choose not to give that power over me, Talbot will have to do."

"Okay, now that were friendly with one another would you cut me down." Sofi's voice was angry and with good reason.

"No, I need you for something, your ability allows you to see what is. You can see the unseen, you can see the truth behind the lies. It works beyond just sight even, you sense when something is a lie and just know what is and what isn't. It is really a shame that language is so limited that it can't truly express what you can do."

Sofi focused her eyes on him, this stranger knew a lot about her and even knew more about her power than she did by the sound of it. "What am I?"

"Special, special beyond words. You have a gift, a gift so few people would ever be lucky enough to have or even know about."

Talbot stepped out of the shadows. He looked like an older man that still looked pretty young with a few gray hairs on the side of his head. He wore a simple black suit and tie making him look like a proper English gentleman. His face had a warm and calm smile that could make you believe everything would be all right.

Talbot continued to smile at her, "You can tell, correct? I am not lying to you."

"I don't know." Sofi said unsure about anything. "You might be able to do something with you magic."

"I am a giant pink elephant." Talbot sighed.

It wrong, that's how it worked, whenever someone lied to her Sofi just felt something was wrong no matter how small or how truthful the lie sounded. "Okay, maybe you're not lying."

"In the magical world there is a concept of balance, so let's do this: we trade one question for a question. I answer one and you answer one."

Sofi carefully thought about all the things she could ask him, all the questions of her powers that she could finally have answer to and realized there was only one thing she really needed to know. "Where are my friends?"

"Your reapers are safe and sound. I have them locked up in another part of this special building. Some of my people wanted to kill them the second they arrived but I told them no. I put them in a binding circle, in all honesty I was interested in seeing what will happen with them." Talbot clapped his hands together. "Now, about these reapers, what do the reapers know about mine and my cabal's plan?"

"Plan? They don't know anything, I don't know anything. I just ran into them for the first time today when I was attacked. I was just lucky."

Talbot studied her for a moment as thinking over if she really was telling him the truth. "Destiny is a funny thing." Talbot chuckled to himself.

"Where are we?" Sofi focused on trying to find out everything she could about the place and maybe she could find away to escape.

"I think you will find this interesting, we are under the border of Austria and Hungary. I do mean under. This entire complex is built under the border. You see, during the cold war the people of Hungary dug out tunnels to help people escape into the neighboring country." Talbot paused for a moment. "Did your father ever tell you about it? No, of course not you have been too young." Talbot looked at her for a moment and then answered a question she never asked. "During the Soviet control over Hungary there was a revolution and the Soviets attacked. From the news that managed to escape it wasn't pretty. When your father was young and took up working with his hands to repairing homes to help fend for himself and his family. I personally think that's why he wanted to be a painter, to see beauty in anything. At the very least it gave him skill as a construction worker to help pay the bills when painting failed." Talbot paused watching how she took in the news. "I'm sorry, it must be unpleasant to think about. Let me answer your question, some Hungarians managed to make a few escape tunnels from Hungary to Austria and keep it secret. After the Iron Curtain that kept the borders blocked came down the tunnels were buried and forgotten. A few years ago I stumbled upon them and remodeled them a little all in secret."

Sofi didn't know her father too long and didn't know his life history and this piece of information was just another thing Talbot knew that she didn't.

"What are you planning?"

"Let me show you." Talbot moved closer to her and placed his face front of hers. "Wizard, witches and other powerful magic users can use a skill. A skill that can be rather intense. When one uses this ability they can see a person's essence or soul. What they see lingers in them for the rest of their lives. I imagine with your abilities and mine to focus it a little it should explain everything."

Talbot focused his eyes as he stared down into her eyes. Sofi felt a wave of something wash over her. That was when she saw nothing but darkness.

Safi

Talbot

目
何色がいいかの？

Chapter 06: Talbot

Sofi found herself in the darkness. What that meant was beyond her understanding. She didn't seem to feel anything, like she wasn't standing on anything or flying or being suspended but she simply was.

But she wasn't alone. A ball of light made of white mist glowed in the darkness. It hung in front of her. She looked at it and just knew it was Talbot, that was the very essence of Talbot and there was nothing more Talbot than that. She didn't understand it but she was gazing upon his soul, or as much as her human and somewhat limited mind could perceive. All she could guess is that the ability he was talking about was letting her see this. She saw his light and she got a feeling for who he was which was expected from a human. The thing was she had an ability that wasn't normal to humans and allowed her to see more, that was what Talbot was counting on.

Events started to unfold before her and she saw what he wanted him to see. Talbot wanted her to see his story. The darkness was replaced with colors, lights and sounds.

Like many other stories his started with his birth. Talbots own birth. Sofi watched as a tired woman in a cottage laid in a small bed cradling a small baby in her arms. The cottage was humble and small. Sofi got a sense that it was a long time ago but didn't know how long ago, she only guess that it was sometime in the dark ages. She wasn't a history expert but she had seen enough movies that took place during that time to get an idea of the old clothing. They were little more than rags, old hand made dresses.

The room was silent except for the cries of a baby. That was when Sofi realized that the woman looked tired, more tired than any other person she had ever seen. That was when Sofi realized she wasn't tired but dying, Sofi was watching as the life drained from her body.

    An old woman with a wrinkled skin walked in with a mournful look on her face, she knew what was happening. The mother looked at her baby with a smile and kissed him on his forehead.

    The mother spoke with a tired voice, "Please take care of him for me."

    "Of course." The old woman promised her.

    The old woman had helped her give birth and tended to her as best as she could but in the end there was no fighting it. Neither the old woman or even Sofi knew when it happened but it did, the woman had died with her baby still crying in her arms. It took a moment but the woman pulled the baby from the dead woman's arms.

    That was the start of Talbot's life and the end of his mother's. She had been sick for a long time and most would have called it a miracle that she managed to bring that child into the world. Some will focus on her death and see this as a sad story but the old woman didn't. The old woman saw that as a beautiful story of a woman who gave her son life despite loosing her own. The Old woman raised the boy and tried to make him see it as she did but he only focused on his mother's death.

    The old woman was a witch, not a terribly powerful one but she had her gifts. She used her power to heal people and only asked for what they could afford. She raised the boy as best she could and showed him how to tap into the natural power of the world.

    That was when the world changed around Sofi, changing to help tell her the story. The baby had grown up to be a ten year old boy and sat in front of the old woman who sat under a large tree in a field. Sofi felt the warm summer sun touching her face and a warm breeze run past her. It seemed so real that she almost forgot it was a memory.

    The old woman continued her lesson to the boy as he listened, "We are all connected. This whole world and every living thing are connected. There is energy and that connects us, some of us call it magic, some call it mana, and some just call it the life force. It runs through our bodies and our world. They call them ley lines and they are like rivers of the Earth's own natural power that cross all over the world, like how our own veins carry blood they carry power and life all around the world. Many people naturally draw the power from nature and others know how to tap into these lines and tap into this power. "

The young Talbot asked the woman, "What can you do with that power?"

"Almost anything, the real question is if should it be done."

"I don't understand."

"You're young and I don't think you have to understand it yet. Power like that is different, it connects us, remember? When I die my body will become one with the Earth. My life force will fade away and the world will take it. "

Talbot gave her a scared look like she had told him the worst thing ever.

She chuckled at his look, "No, don't give me that look. Don't look at it like it was something terrible."

"You just told me that you will just stop being."

She sighed shaking her head, "No, don't think about it like that. My body and my energy will break down and feed into the world. They don't just vanish, they will be taken by the world and be taken for others. My body will feed the Earth and the Earth will use that to feed the plants and in turn feed the animals who will feed people. My death will give others life, others have died so that I could have the gift of life. Even then I won't be gone. My physical body and my energy will continue on in this cycle but not my soul. My soul will be carried to another place and there I will continue my own path."

"Carry you? What carries you away and to where?"

"I don't know exactly know where but I have an idea of who."

The old woman told him the stories of reapers.

For years the woman slowly taught him about magic. Then things changed. When he was seventeen years old the old woman went to the forest and was found by witch hunters. Witch Hunters were people who usually thought magic was evil and used to summon evil things into the world. There is magic for that and usually those that do that magic do terrible things just to cast it but she never dared do any of the sort. They simply feared magic and blindly hunted anyone they thought might do it.

One night he wandered into the forest and found a large fire burning and right in the middle of it he found the bodily remains of the old woman. He didn't know how long he stood by the fire and watched it in horror, all he knew was by the time he let what happen sink in the fire had gone out.

Sofi watched it unfold and watched a boy weep for the only mother he ever knew.

The following years flew past her, she watched him grow up and continued his secret studies. He studied all he could on the reapers and discovered things about their master. He discovered books with secrets. He discovered a way to spare his life. All he had to do was stand in the right spot on a ley line during right time to allowed himself to draw energy from the ley line into himself and use it as his own life force to give himself several more years. It slowed his aging to almost nothing, in centuries he only aged a couple of decades. The world changed around him, Kingdoms and empire fell and farmers became workers in factories. He watched the world grow old. He met people and watched them grow old and die. Sometimes he loved them and sometimes he hated them but one by one he watched them all die. Wars engulfed the world and whole continents became killing fields. After the war fear spread throughout the world and more war came and with it more death. All he started to see was death and that was when he stopped dealing with the living. He saw no point in making new relationships if he would lose them to death. Alone he wandered and he saw all his loses, all the trouble and wars, would all be nothing without death. That was when he came up with an idea to stop Death itself. Maybe it was years of being alone and focused on all the death in the world that made it seem like a good idea. So he made his plans alone and waited.

In the last few years he finally found what he needed to do but he would need help. He searched the world for wizards, mages, witches, sorcerers, magicians and every type of magic user to carry out his plan. He carefully searched the world for those who would agree with his plan. He found a place underground that could be hidden filled with echoes of peoples running trying to escape fear and death as they did. Then he found a person with an ability that he needed. Sofi watched it all happen.

With a flash of light Sofi snapped back into the real world as Talbot pulled away.

Sofi felt warm tears streaming down her face. "What is your plan?"

Talbot fixed his tie as he looked at her, "Pardon? I showed you everything, you should know what my plan is."

"I know, I know, I just have to hear it."

He smiled kindly at her, "I plan to conquer. I plan not to end the idea but the actual being. I will bind death and claims all its power for myself and my followers. I will replace death. I will stand above humanity, above spirits, above the reapers, above the beasts, above the monsters, above magicians, above even gods and above all that lives and dies. I will end death and make the world better for it. I will make the world into one where no one needs to die."

Sofi shuddered at the words.

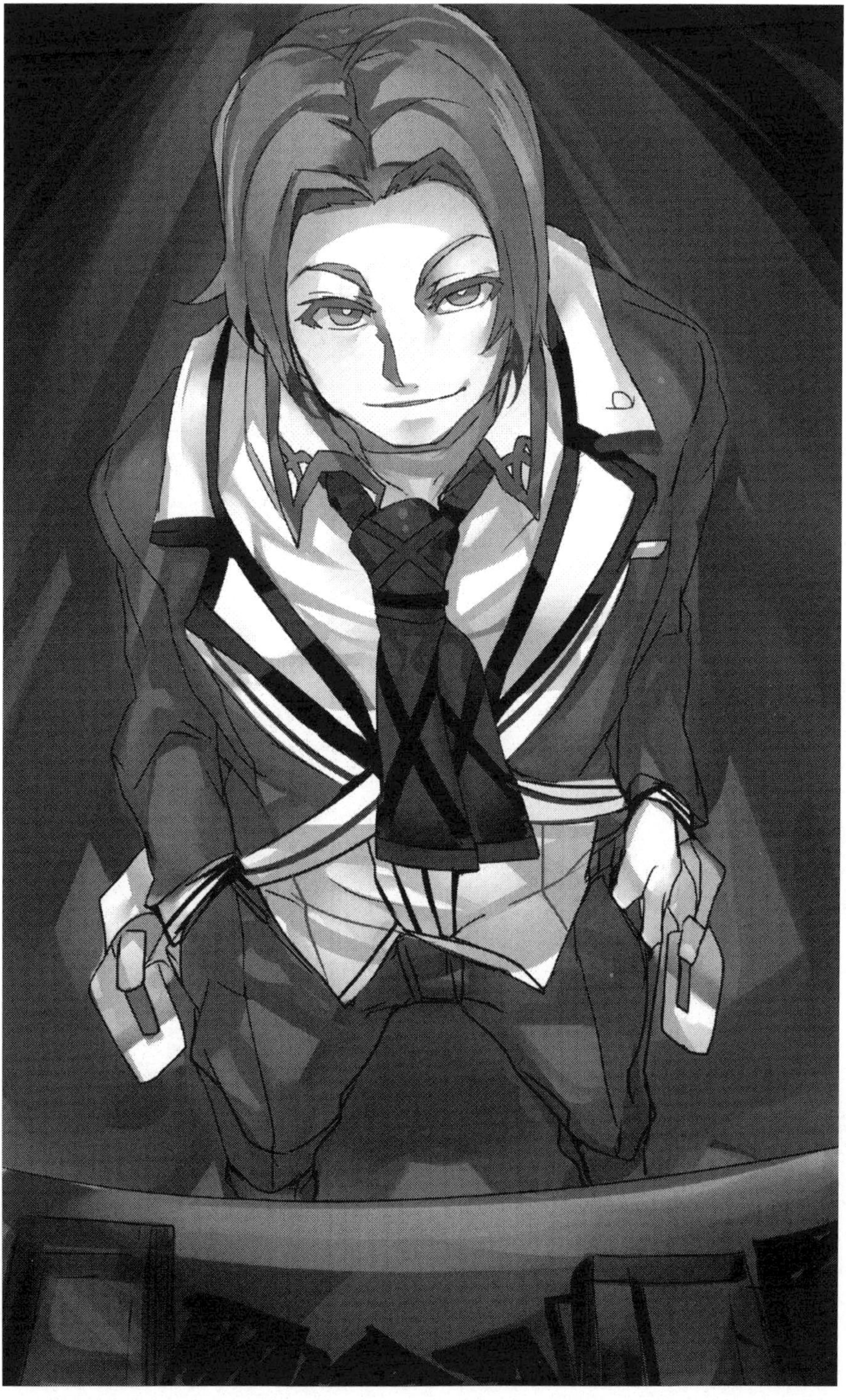

Chapter 07: Lightning Of The Gods

Valdis crashed into a wall. She didn't know if the cracking sound was the wall or her our bones. Then Valdis felt her bones start to mend and put themselves in place so she assumed it was a little bit of both. She could heal quickly but the more injuries she took the more energy she used up and the longer it would take for the next injury to heal. She normally wouldn't worry too much about it except she still hadn't recovered all the energy she had used up earlier that day and getting hit a lot wasn't helping.

Her head was shaking as the woman walked towards her.

Maeva looked at her, "You're not as powerful as you were when you first attacked us."

"You hurt my friend." Valdis spat out the words. "I had to use a lot of energy to keep him on this side of the veil."

Maeva's voice was detached, "It seems like such a wasted effort, he will soon be pushed to the other side and not too long after you will join him."

Valdis didn't like the sound of that, her grip grew tighter on the sword and she jumped at the magician. Valdis slashed at the woman but the instant that the sword hit the full force of the attack bounced off and slammed back onto her.

Valdis crashed into the wall again and coughed spitting out black blood.

"Have you not figured it out yet?" Maeva taunted her. "It's the hand, it protects me. It will reflect any attack and turn it back on the attacker."

Valdis sighed, she was tired and she had lost a lot of energy but she mustered what she could and quickly teleported behind her. Grabbing the sword tight she slashed at her again hoping that if Maeva couldn't see the attack or react in time she could get one hit in. The sword touched the magician again only for the attack to launch her back down the tunnel.

"I do not have to see it, it does it by itself." Maeva turned to Valdis.

Valdis didn't know what else to do and crawled into the shadows. She wasn't sure she had the power to teleport away again. Even if she could escape Valdis wouldn't dare leave Pax behind.

* * * *

Speaking of which, Pax was in trouble.

"Hello again." Pax said nervously.

Bronte had most of his face covered by his cloak but his smile wasn't covered and it was unsettling but not as much as the sparks shooting off his hand.

Bronte took a step forwards and Pax took a step back, the reaper let out a hiss as his sides hurt from the last attack.

Bronte started to talk to him, his voice suggested he was really going to drag this out and taunt him. "I wanted to kill you the moment we caught you. My boss wanted to talk to you but neither one of you were getting up in time so he moved on to the girl."

"Sofi?" Pax spoke out loud.

"Yeah, we really pushed you three to the last minute. Time is important and you just didn't want to help."

Pax could hear the anger in this voice, he decided to try to get him to continue talking because as long as he was talking he couldn't try and kill him. "Sorry about that."

"Then I didn't get the chance to kill you, you know what it would mean to me to kill a reaper?"

"That's got to be big."

"Like you wouldn't believe. He wanted to have you two in case he needed you to use as leverage against the girl and he just wanted to know how effective the binding circle was when the ritual got started."

"What ritual?" Pax couldn't help but wonder out loud.

* * * *

Back in the dark room Sofi stared at Talbot.

"That's insane." Sofi told him her opinion of his plan.

"Yes, I will admit that trying to bind death itself does sound a little outrages but after time I did manage to figure a way to do it. All binding ritual are basically the same all that is needed is a few minor changes on the symbols depending on what you want to bind. The ankh, the trifold knot, the symbol of eternity all have connections to death. All I needed to do is to find how to reenforce the binding circle for something so massive and powerful."

"Insane! Just crazy!"

"Reapers, all connected to death and its power. My cabal has spread all around the world to points of power and connections of great death. We unleash a massive binding spell all around the world and capture every reaper on the planet. Then we shall connect them all through ley lines and used their power and the planet's power to form a massive binding circle and summon. It will capture death and use its own power that is in the reapers to bind it."

"That is so crazy." Sofi just couldn't stress how crazy the idea was.

"Then the ritual will continue and while death personification is bound the power will be torn form them and shared amongst me and my cabal."

"Do you know how crazy that is?" Sofi yelled at him. At this point she couldn't help but wonder if she had some sort of mental break down and this was all an illusion. Honestly she thought it might have been better if it was.

"You are being very rude." Talbot sounded insulted.

Sofi was speechless for a second. "You are insane. You are about to use people and used them to capture death."

"People? Do you mean the reapers? Why do you care? They aren't people. They're just tools created by death and that I plan to use against it."

"They're not tools!" Sofi couldn't understand what he was saying, she understood the words but not the idea behind them.

"They're people like you and me just a little different."

Sofi didn't know Pax and Valdis long but she didn't want anything to hurt them. If Pax and Valdis were anything like the other reapers she didn't want them hurt either. They weren't human and that she understood that but in many ways they were perfectly human; reapers had goals, dreams, they cared about one another, they cried for one another and they could even love one another and they could feel pain. Everything she heard and saw made her think that what they would go through would be horrible and that was something no one should go through.

"I'm sure you'll understand afterwards." Talbot continued.

"Yeah, that's the thing I don't get. Why did you go through all this trouble to get me?"

"Its simple, it's because we can't see reapers. You can, you can see past the veil and see them even if they try and hide. You are the last part of the ritual, you will focus the power onto the reapers. Your power can pick up on the reaper when are spells can't. Without you and your power the spell, this plan, none of this would be possible all because of you we can target the reapers. Thank you."

He clapped his hands twice and with that torches on the four corners of the room lit up the darkness that filled the room. Painted on the walls were symbols that Sofi couldn't guess what they did. On the wall behind her and the walls to her sides stood giant circles with complicated symbols meant to control and focus her power into the larger ritual about to start around the world.

"I want to apologize before I start." Talbot sounded actually sorry about this part. "I can only imagine this will be agony for you."

Sofi was silent for a moment, that is why they never asked her just to come in because no one sane would volunteer for the pain that she was going to be forced into. She had seen most of the plan and her power allowed her to know it was true, that's why he left this part out because Talbot didn't want her to panic anymore than she needed to because he was trying to be kind.

* * * *

Back in the dark tunnel Pax tried to come up with some idea to escape the magician. He took a step back slowly. He didn't really have anywhere to run as he was in a tunnel. The most he could do is try and buy himself time and hope something changed, something small or anything changed that would give him a chance to escape.

"Why am I even talking?" Bronte shook his head. "I'm just going to kill you, Maeva is probably already done killing your girl and even if we need reapers I'm sure two won't make much of a difference."

At that moment Pax lost hope. Bronte stretched out his hands and electricity formed and arched between his fingers. He moved his hands and the lightning swayed between them. His every moment lead the lightning along and as his hands pushed forwards the lightning followed until they exploded out of his reach and towards the reaper. The lightning as it left his hands lit the area around them with it's white-blue light.

Pax could feel the heat coming off the lightning as it moved towards him but he felt something else just a second before that. He felt a wave of power like what he felt right before he meet Sofi, that same sensation of magic moving and changing the world. That feeling is what made him throw himself to the ground at the very last second letting him dodge the attack. He closed his eyes but the heat wave rushed over him as the lightning passed over head and towards the darkness of the tunnel. The lights over head flicked off and on as the lightning was released.

He heard Bronte take a step forward and he knew he was in trouble, he could try to crawl away but on the floor he couldn't dodge another attack. Pax had only managed to buy himself a few more seconds, those seconds were valuable and that was all he needed. He felt the same feeling and felt the heat of lightning again at first he thought the magician was attacking again but he realized it was coming from the wrong direction. As impossible as it would seem his own attack was coming back to him and maybe it was surprise but he didn't act in time and Bronte was throw backwards by the lightning. Bronte's body shock for a second before the pain became too much and he passed out.

"Huh?" Valdis crawling on the floor came into the light of the hanging light bulb above them.

"What?" Pax replied.

"That idiot." Maeva annoyed said.

What had happened was simple, both reapers were on the ground and the lightning was shot in a way that it quickly passed over them. The attack would continue to go for a while unless it hit something and the only target in its range was Maeva just down the tunnel but thanks to her new hand attacks didn't work on her. The attack Bronte sent hit her body but was bounced back down the tunnel where it hit a very surprised Bronte.

Pax wished he could say he planned it and Valid wished to say that was why she was crawling but really they just got lucky.

"Now I'll just take care of the two of you and get him some help for his wounds." Maeva snarled at the pair.

The way her new found power worked was basically redirecting forces, so if something attacked it would be redirected back. Now what this means when she punches sometimes all the force of the impact gets pushed back too including what force would normally hit her fist. It allowed her to basically ignore the Newton's Third law of motion and double the strength of her attacks. Her hand formed a fist and slammed right down. If it wasn't for Valdis fast reflexes it would have hit her instead of the floor. The whole tunnel seemed to shake and spiderweb like cracks formed around the crater that as made by her punch. Small shattered stones were tossed about and Valid noted how one pebble was throw at Maeva's face by the force of the attack only to be bounced back with a greater force. The other broken pieces of stone bounced around the tunnel. Valdis squinted as some of the shattered stone bits hit her.

Valdis blinked and for a split second she saw something, a

small dirty cut on Maeva's face. It was a small faint cut that if the light didn't hit it in just the right way Valdis wouldn't notice and if she hadn't noticed it was fresh she would have brushed it off as nothing.

Valdis grabbed Pax with one hand and gripped her sword with her free hand and jumped up. When both of them were on their feet she looked at Pax from the corner of her eyes watching Maeva stand straight and glare at them. Valdis let the familiar black mist energy coat her blade.

"Pax, do you trust me?" Valdis asked the other reaper.

"Yes." Pax didn't hesitate to answer.

"Thank you." Valdis smiled at the answer. "I need you to punch her."

"What?"

"Punch her." Valdis gripped the sword tighter.

"Are you trying to get him killed?" Maeva teased them. "Any attack will just bounce off me and go back. Have I tossed you around so much you've damaged whatever excuse for a brain you have?"

Valdis let her eyes narrow as she focused on her task. The situation was this, he was going to get hurt but Pax did trust Valdis so he had to trust that she had a good reason for letting him get hurt.

"I trust you." Pax whispered and he rushed forwards and punched her.

Pax wasn't a fighter by anyones definition. The last time he threw a punch was when he meet a boxer who fought in an underground boxing ring in 1920s Manhattan. Everyone told the boxer that if he went into the ring to fight the champion he would die and they were right. Pax went to collect the boxer's spirit but when he wasn't ready to leave the boxer showed Pax how to throw a punch. Pax took a step forwards and swung his right fist right at her face. Maeve made no motion to block the attack, she wouldn't have to. Pax was scared, he knew this would hurt him but out of the corner of his eye he saw Valdis with her sword ready to run her through.

His fist collided with her face but her face didn't show any sign of her feeling it or even the punch connecting and a split second later Pax felt the force double back on his fist. Pax tried to stifle a moan as he was sure his wrist just broke. That was when he noticed the magician frozen in pain.

He pulled his fist away and looked over and saw Valdis with her sword through Maeva's chest.

Valdis huffed, "You can only block one attack at the time."

The light bulb above them had been swinging around wildly since the fight had started, throwing shadows around, and it started to steady. Pax noticed tiny stones and dust over the magician's arm.

Valdis continued, "I saw one little rock bounce off you when you punched but the others and the dust still hit you, you just didn't notice."

"Wait, is that why you told me to attack?" Pax said holding his hurt wrist.

"I was thinking about attacking together." Valdis said holding the sword still. "You reacted a little faster than I thought and I stabbed her when your attack was being bounced back. So, I guess that was good timing. It worked."

Maeva opened her mouth letting her breath escape as she tried to talk.

Valdis tired of the woman pushed the sword's entire blade through her and a flicker of light from it shimmered as her spirit popped out. On the very tip of the sword was the spirit, looking just like the now empty body, Maeva look in shock at her body. For a slight moment Pax wondered if things like these were what people talked about in battlefield when people said they were hurt that they stood above their bodies.

Anger dripped of the reaper's words, "You attacked my friend, you attacked me and then trapped us!" Valdis gave her a glare that made Pax shiver. "Listen to me when I tell you this: Go to hell!" Valdis with one swift motion pulled out the sword and the

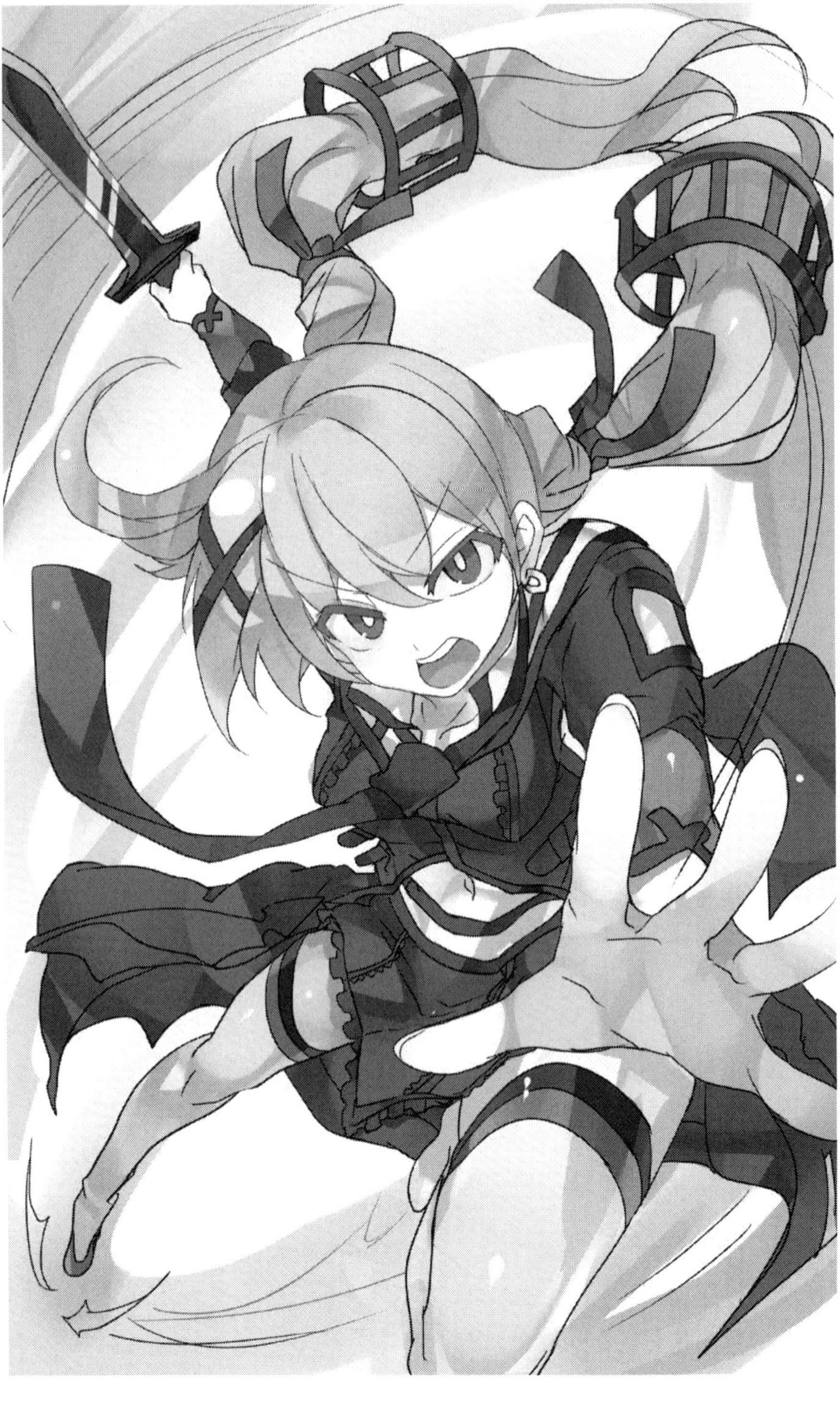

soul was ripped back into the body.

The body showed no sign that it had been stabbed it just looked paler and her eyes just looked clouded before it collapsed onto the floor.

"Did you kill her?" Pax couldn't help but ask.

"No, I just ripped out her soul for a few seconds." Valdis let the black energy wash away from the sword. "And then just put it back in backwards." Valdis looked at the body on the floor as it twitched. "Physically she's fine but I have to imagine on a spiritual level it hurt a lot and I'm not sure she will ever be able to move her body again."

Valdis put her sword away.

"It would have been a perfect plan if my wrist didn't break." Pax told her.

"Let me see." Valdis grabbed his hand and moved it around in the circle and judged his reaction. "Oh, that's not a break, at best that's a sprain. I don't think you even hit her that hard."

"It hurt, that's what I know."

Valdis picked up his hand to her lips and gently kissed his wrist. Pax watched that same black mist like energy escape her kiss and slowly sunk into his skin. It only took a second before Pax felt the pain leave him as her energy started to mend his injuries. It was just a little energy focused right at the injury putting everything back in place. If he hand't been part reaper it was likely this trick wouldn't work.

"You don't have to do that." Pax worried about her. "You already used up a lot of your energy. I don't think you should just be giving it away like that."

"Don't worry I know what I'm doing." Valdis pulled away and looked up to him giving him a bright smile. "Let's go find your new friend and save her."

"Her name is Sofi."

"Yeah, I'm sorry I'm just not good at remembering names and it's been a crazy day.

* * * *

Sofi was scared, more scared that she had been in her entire life. Talbot pulled out an old silver pocket watch and looked over the time. He went over to a table that held all sorts of tools and grabbed an old clay jar. He walked over to her and stopped right in front of her where a circle had been drawn.

"There are not a lot of things that can carry a soul." Talbot explained to her with a touch of regret in his voice. "We had a man in our cabal looking into that, his name was Redgrove. Sometime back he had stumbled onto his jar that could contain souls. The problem was that we didn't have a soul to put into. That was when he found a reaper but things got out of hand and he let information out. There are penalties for doing that and in the end...."

"In the end what?" Sofi questioned the man.

"We needed a soul and he thought he could use reapers to get the knowledge to get one but when he failed we made him the soul that we'd use." Talbot pulled the lid off and inside the jar was a ball of brilliant light almost screaming at the world.

"Please stop." Sofi begged.

The soul that was Redgrove clinging to life and kept safe in the jar and kept from forming a proper spirit or even warping into a ghost, inside the jar it was kept in pain not by choice only because it didn't have a body anymore.

Talbot spoke softly, "This is the last part. A still living soul, one that doesn't know death. At this exact moment my cabal is all over the world getting ready for me to do this. There will be no turning back."

"Please! I'm begging you, please stop!" Sofi in a panic tried to rip the ropes off.

"I'm sorry, I really am but this has to happen."

"Why?" Sofi yelled, tears started to stream from her eyes.

"When this is done no one will ever have to die again. No one will need to be afraid of loosing those they love or have them taken away. There will be no murders, no disaster to be afraid of. I promise you it will be worth it."

"No!"

"It has to happen." Talbot told her. "Look at it. I made my base here in the border of the nations that happen to be the nation of your parents. While you ran you actually moved towards here. Redgrove swore that he faced two reapers a pale man and a girl with silver hair. They didn't know anything, out of every creature in this or any world they were the ones to show up again. Destiny is binding us all together, all to be here on this day. This is meant to happen."

Talbot started to chant in a language that Sofi couldn't even pretend to know. Sofi struggled to escape as hard as she could. Talbot turned over the jar and let the soul out and the circle beneath it started to glow white. That soul was what would power the ritual.

The symbols above Sofi's head started to glow bright blue and her head felt like it was cracked open. No matter how hard she tried she only focused on reapers. In her mind she saw Pax with his kind smile, Valdis holding the sword like a proper warrior, of Thanatos and his black wings when he came for her parents and the image of the skeleton with a black robe and scythe. Sofi started to scream as the pain spread across her body.

* * * *

All around the world people from the cabal started to chant their own part in the ritual at that time. In Japan there was a forest called Aokigahara and in that forest magicians gathered in a circle with symbols around them. None of them showed any sign but winds gathered around them and moans filled the air as the ritual woke the ghost of people who died there and refused to move on or follow a reaper.

In the desert called Death Valley the cabal waited for the moment and started to chant on the spot where several wagon trains full of families met their end.

In Greenwich London a group of wizards and magicians

gathered at a local college. They hide under the library and started to chant at the same time as everyone else. The school sat on a powerful ley line they wanted to tap into.

All over the world on places where people died, where there had been great death, terrible battles, terrible disasters and places of power the cabal gathered and started to chant all at the same second.

The sky turned dark, all over the world until the sky was pitch black. At that moment people came up with their own reason to believe the sky went black. Some said a storm was coming, that their watches were wrong, or it just got dark early that time of year. Still, there were people who sensed energy shifting and that something like the sky going black meant something bad. Organizations that dealt with magic and the supernatural moved to stop the cabal as quickly as possible. Some managed to get to these spots quickly but found the cabal had set up traps, shields and creatures there to guard them. They wouldn't hold them off forever but it would buy them the time they needed.

In front of the Great Pyramids of Egypt a group gathered and started to chant in the sand. Like thunder crashing Anubis arrived and let out a roar.

"Who dares!" Anubis was angry and his tone was enough to shake the very souls of those who heard him.

Anubis had sensed something started to cause the veil to waver and came to investigate. He stood in between the members of the cabal chanting and got closer than anyone else for one reason, he was meant to. Reapers started to appear around him.

Circles filled with symbols formed around the groups from the cabal all over the world. Anubis read the symbols and the meaning behind them and it scared him in ways he didn't think he could be scared anymore. He tried to escape, but it was too late. The circles glowed with the same bright light of the soul.

The magic circles acted the same way souls who needed reapers acted, they made the same ripples and called every reaper in the world and forcibly pulled them towards the circles. Anubis screamed as his body fell apart and turned into a black cloud and was forcibly pulled into the circle along with the other reapers. This happened at every gathering all over the world.

* * * *

In the tunnel Valdis screamed as she felt herself being forcibly pulled away.

"I'm being pulled away." Valdis clung to Pax in pain. "Something is happening! Something is very wrong!"

Maybe it was because she used a lot of her reaper energy, maybe it was because she was close to the center of the overall spell and just far enough from any major gathering but Valdis wasn't being pulled away as strongly as the others.

Valdis screamed in pain as tears forced their way out of her eyes. "Please make it stop!"

Pax watched as Valdis flickered between her body and her true form of a black cloud. Pax noted a small can of paint by one of the wall, he knew it had to be what they had used to make the circle in the first place. He begged to whatever force in the universe was listening that this worked. He grabbed a paint brush on the side of the bucket and dipped it into the black paint and grabbed Valdis. Valdis flickered and he forced her into the circle. With the paint brush he filled in the gaps in the circle he made with the sword.

Valdis moaned in pain but settled back on her human form. Pax wrapped his arms around her as she continued to shake, Valdis felt like some terrible wave was washing over her, a wave that was washing over the whole world.

* * * *

Back in the other room Sofi screamed in pain. She just wanted the pain over with but couldn't do anything but scream. To describe it like her body was set on fire would have been putting it mildly and worst of all it wasn't stopping.

All over the world reapers were being caught in bidding spells and being broken down to their most basic forms, broken down into energy. All that energy was captured and tunneled and moved around the world all at once forming on the veil around the Earth a massive binding circle. Around world places began to shake, storms appeared out no where and some of the smaller volcanoes erupted. Animals all over the world panicked but people who were so detached from nature didn't notice it happen.

Sofi didn't hear it over her screams the ceiling exploded when the spell was finished and black lightning fell through it hitting Talbot.

Sofi gasped hopping that it was finally over. Talbot stood up and coughed. "I'm sorry that hurt." Talbot started to walked forward towards Sofi. "I am going to assume that you expected to die. I told you that once it was over no one would die, that included you, I am just happy that you survived it long enough to make it to the end."

Sofi forced herself to lift her head, "You look different." Sofi corrected herself, "No, you are different."

Talbot's skin was paler and his hair was blacker and his eyes were nothing but black orbs. Talbot also now had the faint smell of dead lilacs. Sofi looked to her side to the circles on the walls that glowed with black light. What scared her was that the light seemed to be screaming in pain just silently enough that you might not notice the screams.

"All the reapers in creation are kept in those special bidding circle." Talbot explained in a dreamy tone. "These bidding circles are keeping the whole system in place and holding their boss right between the Veil and this world." Talbot looked up. "That must be why the sky has gone black. Still, death's power remains and is shared between me and my followers." Talbot looked at Sofi. "It is strange, I'm not sure what I expected it to feel but this is just indescribable."

Sofi felt him reach over and his cold hand stroked her face and she gasped. Suddenly all the pain vanished and she felt whole. Any injury that she suffered because of the ritual or any tiredness she felt were gone. A fog seemed to float over her mind making the pain seem less as she looked back on the memories of only a moment ago.

"There." Talbot said softly. "All better now. I know I hurt you but only because I had no other choice. I am sorry my child but wake up and get ready to meet a new world."

The ropes around her fell apart and she was free and her feet touched the ground. Talbot smiled at her, he smiled like a man who had become a god or a man who thought himself a god at least.

Sofi who saw, heard, felt, sensed and knew things were either true or not knew what he was. He was wrong. She saw a man and saw what he had become was distorting the world around him. She sensed nature crying out in pain by his presence.

There are words for people like him but the only one that came to Sofi's mind was that he was just wrong.

Chapter 08: A Deathless World

Valdis cried in his arms. "I don't feel her anymore."

"What?" Pax asked her as he took the sword and broke the circle again.

The whole thing had ended for them when black lightning ripped through the roof hitting the magicians. Neither magician seemed to wake from the attack but still didn't seem dead.

Valdis didn't pay attention to them, "I never notice it before but she has always been there and now she isn't."

"Who?"

"Our Lady, Death, she's gone."

"What?"

"You're not a reaper at the moment. You don't have a connection to her power right now but I just felt her vanish."

"Valdis, listen to yourself if something happened to Death everyone would know the moment it happened."

"She's not there anymore. I know it, she's not." Valdis put her face in her hands. "Something is wrong, I don't know what is wrong but something is wrong. We really need a champion right now."

"Yeah, we always do. Where is the blue coated minder of our boss and her husband? Or that time guy?"

"I don't know."

In certain circles there are stories of Champions, of heroes and protectors. The stories go that when terrible disasters happen that shake the world or put life in danger someone gets called and becomes a champion. Some have great power or great bravery. They are all brought to the right place at the right time by events so that they are there to stop something from happening or end it. Some become great heroes and legends are told about them for centuries. For whatever reason a force like destiny chooses someone and they go fight the good fight or slay the monster or stop the disaster and most of they time they manage to do it no matter how impossible it seems. The reapers didn't see anyone like that at the moment so they had reason to be worried.

"How about Hercules?" Pax suggested.

"No, I'm pretty sure he's dead." Valdis told him.

"King Arthur?"

"Asleep on the Island of Avalon." Valdis sighed, "I was actually supposed to pick him up but someone stopped his death and just let him sleep."

"Do we have the phone number of a champion or any available hero?"

"Sorry no."

They both tried to play it off but one thing or another they felt that thing had gotten dangerous. They both looked down the dark tunnel, there was something on the other end they didn't need to have power of a reaper to sense it.

Valdis gulped, "I know something happened. I just don't feel her anymore, but she was always there and you just don't notice until she was gone. If something happened to her we have to try and help."

"Spoken like a hero." Pax looked over to her with a gleam of a look in his eyes. "Whenever something bad like this destiny or whatever makes things happen so a champion shows up and I think that's you."

"What? Me?"

"Why not? You're the reaper of heroes, you have the heart of one and you have that sword. Besides you've been saving me this entire day, you've always been my hero."

Secretly Valdis had wondered if she had what it took to be a hero. She had met many and saw what happened to them so it was natural for her to wonder. Part of her never wanted to find out if when it came down to it she could be a hero. There was a lot of responsibility being a hero and she wondered if she could actually carry the burden and the lives at stake.

* * * *

At one end of the tunnel Sofi stared at the man who would be god.

"You can't do this!" Sofi tried to reason with him. "I don't even know where to start. You're trapping countless people."

"Reapers." Talbot felt that he needed to make the difference clear.

"That doesn't matter, I can hear them and they are screaming in pain."

"I simply don't understand you, how can you personify them? They are little more than tools that talk, they're not human so don't mistake them for people."

Sofi massaged her temples in frustration as she realized this argument wasn't going to work on him. Maybe it was her ability or just common sense but something told her that him having this kind of power was wrong. "You just can't have this power. It's not right. No one is supposed to control death."

Talbot shook his head, "That is where you are wrong. I have no intention of controlling death, I just took over their position. I control the forces of death, no one needs to die anymore."

"Then what? The planet is only so big and there is barely enough food for everyone right now. If people don't die we will run out food and places to live. People are still going to get sick and hurt." Sofi didn't want to say it but when she was in pain and screaming she had wished to die than live with that pain for a second longer. "People are going to get hurt, and there are things people aren't supposed to survive through like.... having their head cut off." Sofi knew that was't the best example but she was just trying to keep it together after everything that had just happened.

"I can repair it. I have the power to heal and I can choose who dies and when."

"You can choose who lives and who dies?"

"Yes, I have the power now. There are those who don't

deserve the gift of life and I can take it away. Those who have shown that they deserve it can live forever. Those who don't want to live forever can let me know when they want to die."

"That is so wrong!"

"Wrong? You lost your parents when you were just a child. I can make it so no one has to go through that. No child has to lose their parent anymore."

"No!" Sofi screamed. "Don't bring them up! You know how long I've had to think about them? There isn't a day that goes by that I don't think about them. You know what I have learned? Life isn't fair."

Talbot stared at her, "That is the grand lesson you learned from your parent's death?"

Sofi grit her teeth, "Life isn't fair but its wonderful and the bad thing is that you never know when it's going to end. I have spent my life not focusing on them or even this crazy power I have because I was living. I had a wonderful family in that circus that loved me and I loved them so I ran. I ran to make sure they'd continue to live. The real lesson is that everyone dies, that is fair, we never know when we die but that makes life so precious. That fact makes us live. I lived because I knew that one day I would die. And what is the point if your life never ends, you are just going to take it for granted. And whose to say that you are the best person who pick who gets to live and die?"

"I'm the one who took the right." Talbot voice started to sound less than calm. "I have spent centuries for this day and I will not have some girl whose barely lived two decades lecture me on life and death. I will give you one chance: you can live in this new world and follow the new order or die now and be reunited with your parents."

"New order?"

"I have watched war after war and I don't think canceling out death will stop them. People are scared animals that attack anything that is different. If this is going to work someone has to stop that. Myself and my cabal will take charge and end all conflict. We will make this planet a paradise."

"And anyone who disagrees won't be staying." Sofi gulped at the idea. "You are not the first person to come up with that idea and I look forward to seeing you end up like they did."

At this point he was far more powerful than anyone else and she thought that the forces of the entire world would not be enough to stop him. He could kill her as easy as she took a breath but she couldn't stay quiet and just watch him do such terrible things.

That was when door at the other end of the room opened. Sofi didn't even notice the door earlier because the room was so badly lit but light from the other side of the door way lit it up. Standing in the door way were two figures.

Valdis and Pax looked on at what was before them.

"I know those voices." Pax said looking at the symbols at the walls. "Anubis, Celeste, everyone."

Valdis held the her sword right in front of her. "Don't you feel it. He's somehow got all our Lady's power."

"I really don't want to explain it again." Talbot moaned annoyed. "Long story short: I'm made a special binding spell out of all the reapers and I'm using it hold Death and take their power for myself."

He said that far more casually than anyone else should ever say something like that.

"That's insane!" Valdis yelled.

"I've been trying to explain that." Sofi couldn't help but say.

Valdis glared at the man. " People aren't meant to have that kind of power. Power like that will cloud your mind, power like that will destroy you and destroy the balance of the world."

That has already started. People who died right before the ritual took place had no reapers to lead them to the other side. Everyone else who died who would not normally need a reaper were stuck on this side of the veil without Death pulling them to the other side. Without the influence of Death on the world ghosts who slept started to wake up all over the world. Natural forces like

Earthquakes and storms started to pop up because Death wasn't keeping in check the life forces of the world's ley lines. That was just what was just happening in the first few minutes. Given more time people would start to notice that people weren't dying and then the panic would follow.

"So, I take that the binding circle managed to do it's work and keep you in the spot." Talbot noted to himself. "I suppose my curiosity has paid off. The two of you could be useful to me."

"Like I would ever listen to you!" Valdis screamed at him. " I don't care what you did or why you did it but you're hurting everyone I know and care about. You are destroying the balance of life and death and you're hurting souls. Everything you are doing goes against everything I stand for!"

"I tried to be polite, little reaper." Talbot sighed more annoyed than anything. "I'm going to guess that you agree with her."

Pax knew he was being talked to so he just gave a firm nod.

"It is a shame." Talbot said. "You two are the last reapers and I don't really want to end you all if I didn't have to. I was told by the others that you've caused a lot of trouble." Talbot started to sound detached. "I do think you would cause trouble later. I think this time I'm just going to end the trouble before it even starts." Talbot focused his eyes on Valdis. "You seem like the stronger one. I'm still getting used to this power. Heh, so I've turned off death for everyone so I'm going to try to turn it on just for you,"

Talbot mindlessly pointed his finger at Valdis, the shape of his hand brought to mind the image of a gun and like a gun it brought death. The tip of his finger glowed with that black light before the energy shot out. Time didn't slow down like it does in the movies in fact it all happened quickly, faster than most people realize things happen. That is why it was amazing that things happened the way they did. In a second, in an instant, before Valdis was hit by that attack Pax pushed her out of the way taking it instead. The shot ripped through his chest hitting the wall behind him. The wall crumbled and Pax fell to the ground. Sofi ran past

Talbot and to Pax. Valdis being closer to him managed to get him first and push him onto his back. Valdis quickly tried what she had been doing the entire day and give him some of her energy. Some of her energy pooled in her hand but that was it. She placed her hands over the hole in his chest but after a moment stopped.

She stopped and turned to Talbot. "You! I can't touch him anymore. He's already half dead!"

"Only half?" Talbot said uncaring. "I was trying to kill him all the way."

"I can't touch him! My power already reads him as dead and beyond helping!" Valdis screamed as tears freely flowing from her eyes. She got off the crouching position that she took to check on Pax and picked the sword she tossed away to try and help him.

"Heal him!" Sofi yelled at her.

"I wish I could. His soul is already drifting away." Valdis admitted, her voice cracking as she spoke. "He's dying, his death has been marked and in a little more than a minute he's going to be dead. That is it."

Maybe it was because the pain had cause him to pass out and she wouldn't ever be able to speak to him again and she knew she was going to die soon that Valdis decided to fight. Valdis decided to fight like someone who had nothing to lose because at this point she didn't. Talbot tilted his head to the side as he tried to make sense of the look in Valdis' eyes. The black energy of her that failed to save Pax coiled around the sword. Valdis jumped forwards and cut his head off with one quick slash.

Cutting the head of someone and you'd think would be the end but this wasn't anything normal. The head was tossed into the air by the cut but it stopped and stayed in the air for a few seconds without moving or even falling. Then the head spun in the air and quickly moved back to its body and stuck itself back on.

"Ow! That actually hurt." Talbot rubbed his neck where the cut had been made.

Valdis took a step back not even seeing anything you'd call a scratch on him. Valdis looked at her sword and there wasn't even a drop of blood on it. Valdis sighed, she knew she was going to die but at least she wanted to hurt him and wound him. It seemed like her life wouldn't have that joy. Valdis knew that there wasn't any true purpose to it and it wouldn't make her happy but that didn't matter at all. Valdis just wanted to hurt him as much as possible now.

Valdis stopped thinking and anger filled her mind, body and soul. Valdis put all her energy into moving that sword and using it to cut Talbot as fast and as hard as possible. Blood, bones and everything else was cut from his body and slashed to the side but it stuck in the air and put itself back before the next cut was made. Valdis screamed and yelled and cried out cutting at him.

Sofi as always knew the truth. Sofi watched as Valdis tried to fight, it was meaningless she knew Valdis was hurt and in pain and she just wanted to give that pain to the person who caused it. Sofi understood, all her friends and Pax were taken from her so she understood if Valdis didn't have reason to be safe.

Sofi cried silently not expecting a miracle or anything more so she just couldn't help but cry. What else is someone supposed to do when all hope is gone? That is the thing about hope, when you don't have it is when you need it the most.

Pax was dying, for the second time that day. That had to be some sort of record for a reaper. He didn't know he was going to die when he pushed Valdis out of the way, he didn't even really know she was in danger he just saw the attack coming and reacted. Maybe he did that again when he heard his new friend cry because he gasped and opened his eyes.

"Ah!" Pax tried his best not to scream in pain as his hands reached for anything to grab.

Sofi shook in shock and grabbed his hands, "Pax?"

Pax took a lot of deep breaths trying to make sense of it as he felt his heart beating faster and faster and getting weaker.

Talbot felt his hand stick back into his body and moved his fingers. When he felt his hand he lifted it and pointed at Valdis and shot another blast at her. Valdis slashed at the attack and the attack whirled out of her way hitting the cross that had held Sofi earlier destroying it.

Valdis felt her knees shaking, she had burned up a lot of her power that day and knew that she only had a few minutes before she'd be too tired to move at all. Her body would change back into a small black cloud because she wouldn't have the power to hold the human shape she loved so much. She already was too weak to teleport. She could still move faster and be stronger than people but that meant nothing to someone who wouldn't die.

Pax held onto Sofi's hand breathing as hard as he could, "I'm dying."

That wasn't a reaper talent its just something you know when you are about to die. They say that death tends to focus the mind, that it lets you know what's important and what you have to do with your last moments. It was his last moment and Pax wanted to help his friends.

"Sofi?" Pax gasped.

"Pax? Just relax you're going to be fine." Sofi lied through her teeth.

"You're a terrible liar."

"I know."

"I need you to do something." Pax said between breaths.

Sofi leaned in close as his breathing got harder and his words became softer. "Please move me.... to the wall... to that glowing circle."

"The screaming one?"

"Yes, and do it quickly."

Sofi didn't understand why he wanted that and even Pax wasn't sure but he thought it was the best chance they had and Sofi didn't bother to argue. Sofi took him into her arms as best she could and pulled him along towards the wall.

"I'm sorry." Sofi apologized as she dragged him a long.

"I know." Pax said watching Valdis cut Talbot's hand for what had to be the twentieth time before sticking her sword into his head.

Talbot ripped the sword out of his skull and kicked Valdis in the stomach. He tossed the sword to the side like it was nothing and the black energy just withered away. The kick was a good one and very strong tossing Valdis to the other side of the room and into a wall.

"You little pest." Talbot spat out. "I could have killed you quickly and painlessly but no. You wanted to hurt me and you should be happy you managed to do that. You have also made me angry. I am going to enjoy this. I wonder how long I can keep you alive. I wonder if I can keep you alive as I splatter you across these walls. I'm going to learn to do so much today. I wonder if I can bring back your friend from the other side, maybe then I can kill him again!" Talbot scream and spit escaped his mouth as he did.

Talbot walked slowly to her as if he had all the time in the world. Valdis laid on the ground in pain after she fell off the wall. Talbot grabbed her head with his hand and forced her onto her feet. Her long silvery pig tails had fallen apart and let her long silver hair fall down her back in tangles. A trail of blood formed on her forehead.

"Your blood is black." Talbot mused as he forced Valdis to look him in the eyes and lifted her in the air so her feet dangled. "Or is that just a dark red?"

"Just die." Valdis said weakly her wounds closing very slowly.

"I would say the same to you." Talbot started to crush her head in his hand.

Valdis let out a horrible scream her skull started to crack under Talbot's grip.

They reached the wall and Pax could hear the screams and moans of the reapers trapped in a giant planet wide bidding spell. Pax let his finger touched the hole in his chest letting his fingers collect blood. His hand soon were covered in blood and pressed it against the symbols.

"She's screaming." Pax spoke to the wall. "I'm dying and she's going to join me soon if you don't do something. Do your job! Come for me. Do that and you can stop this!"

Sofi held him as she felt his body get stiff and weak.

They say magic and science are different but in many ways they are exactly the same. Computer circuits are delicate things and they have to be made in perfectly clean rooms because even a little tiny piece of dust can get into them and just ruin them. Those symbols working the same way, they move the power that was the reapers around and get it to do what was needed just like circuits move electricity. The little piece of dust in this case was Pax and his blood. In magic blood is powerful, contains life and can be used to make connections. That little blood of the dying man tapped into the network of reaper energy and spoke them. That blood told them they had someone to collect and that made a connection for them to reach for him. That little touch of blood started to form a crack in the system and reached out the basic nature of the reapers leaving a tiny fault.

It was like a crack in a damn and the whole room started to shake. The symbols on the wall started to flicker on and off. The screaming that came from the symbols was replaced with a loud hum and oddly enough the smell of freshly cut grass and cocoa beans.

"What happened?" Talbot stopped his attack on Valdis looked at the symbols on the walls.

Symbols started to vanish little by little and then they just stopped glowing all at once. Talbot fell to the ground as his body began to shake. Valdis scooted away from him and good thing to because the following second energy ripped out of him in the form of black lightning heading straight for the sky.

Talbot collapsed to the ground his skin regaining it's color. Talbot raised his head to look around just in time to find several clouds of black smoke filling the room. The clouds quickly took on the forms they wanted. Soon the dark figure of the ancient god known as Anubis formed. Talbot tried to crawl away but was stopped as the newly reformed Grim Reaper and Morton formed both holding their scythes and giving him a look that said they were more than eager to use them. Talbot tried to move away but the sound of metal stomping on the ground. Talbot gulped seeing the figure of Marik in his black armor.

The next sound Talbot heard was the sound of twin flintlocks being cocked. Nila stood with her guns pointed at the magician. She now wore a blue pin stripe suit and her red framed glasses glinted as she spoke. "Oh, please give me a reason."

Nearby a new reaper showed up, she was tall with long white hair and shinning blue eyes and wore a long flowing white dress. Valdis was hurt and tossed to the side but this reaper gently stroked her face slowly giving her some of her energy healing her.

"Celeste?" Valdis said her wounds started to heal.

"You need to take better care of yourself." Celeste told her.

A young woman whose kind face reminded people of a caring mother and one with long straight black hair dressed in a white and red shrine maiden outfit helped Valdis get on her feet. A grandmother like reaper handed Valdis back her sword.

Anubis went to Pax, "You did well, you gave us a connection to lead us out. We're all free."

Around the world wherever the cabal was holding the ritual the reapers were freed and were quick to gather around the magicians. Anyone who had been fighting the magicians and had been failing because of their power ups were saved because of this and in return none of them tried to stop the very angry reapers.

In the tunnels a certain creature dragged the unconscious forms of the other two magicians in its jaws. The animal was part lion, part hippo and part crocodile. The head was that of a crocodile with the lions mane so its jaw was long enough to drag both of them over to the other reapers.

"Good work, Ammut." Anubis patted this special reaper on the head.

Dropping the magicians on the ground Ammut went to the side of the dying Pax and let out a whimper.

The jackal faced Anubis looked at Pax. "You made us all proud. You saved us all and this world. Go pass the veil with that knowledge."

"W-wait, do-does that mean" Pax let out a harsh and weak cough. "I was the... champ-pion?" Pax couldn't really make sense of that. "W-who would cho-" Pax coughed again some blood dripping out of his mouth as he did. "Chose me to be champion?"

Anubis explained, "Sometimes the champion chooses themselves. They saw people in danger and they acted to save them."

"Can you help him?" Sofi pleaded with them.

"We can't, he is beyond our ability to help him." Anubis admitted his voice quiet and weak.

The reapers all moved out of Valdis' path to Pax.

"No, please no." Valdis let out.

The air above them shook and the sky was still black but then color swept across the sky in the form of a stream of brightly colored lights.

"Oh god no." Talbot cried out seeing the strange light.

Many people would have thought it was the Northern Light but those lights were not all that scary.

Three bolts of lightning, this time normal looking and not the black ones, struck out from the lights striking the magicians. The lightning avoided the reapers and Sofi and didn't even make the room warmer. The lightning zapped the three magicians and they just sort of dissolved into the light of the electricity before it vanished. The same thing happened all over the world at the same time to every single member of the cabal.

Pax let out a small groan, his breath stopped and the light in eyes vanished. The rest was silence and he was gone.

"It is time." Anubis said in little more than a whisper.

Valdis moved towards him but stopped as someone spoke up, "Valdis you don't have to."

The reapers all turned to the doorway where a bright light shone. They couldn't see the person standing in the door frame only her outline.

All the reapers bowed to her and mumbled in respect, "My

lady."

"Now is not the time for that." Deatz spoke to them. "We all have a lot of work to do. I know you have been through a lot and I will be there to help. Every one please get started as soon as possible. I will deal with this."

Deatz snapped her fingers and everyone went to where they had to be.

Death   Life

Chapter 09: Life

Talbot didn't know where he was. He knew he was alone and somewhere dark. Everything around him was a black and an endless void. As far as he could tell there seemed to be no up or down. He didn't even know if he was standing on anything, it didn't feel like he was standing or floating he simply was in the middle of the darkness. He could see himself with not problem but couldn't see anything else, like there was a special light that only allowed himself to be seen.

Talbot tried to make sense of the situation by remembering what had happened before. All he knew was that he had been caught by the reapers and something hit him. He didn't think he was dead, he certainly never imagined that being dead would feel like this. He wasn't even in pain at most he was a little confused.

Was his punishment going to stay there alone? He was a magician and had trained his mind to be strong so even something like this wouldn't have much of an effect on his mind.

"What do you intend to do to me?" Talbot yelled out into the darkness.

"Do you still think you are in control?"

The voice came out of nowhere and it was a cross between a hiss and a boom. The voice was everywhere.

"You sound like a man?" Talbot spoke out loud.

"Still trying to take control. You think if you can know who I am that you might be able to use that information and turn things around. That's what's wrong with you, you don't change but instead cling to things and how things were. You've been alive for centuries and in the last few centuries people have changed. People have learned that they have to live together instead of trying to fight and conquer each other. To live side by side, for the most part anyway. You on the other hand seem to be stuck in the old way of thinking. You just have to have everything and destroy what you don't want. You even want to take death out of the picture."

"And what's wrong with that?!" Talbot yelled at the voice. "Its human nature to fight and over come death. Every moment of life has to be fought to be kept and I will claw my way back to the world to get even just one more day."

"Yes, rage against the dying of the light. Did you ever actually read the poem? The guy who wrote it tells you to fight to stay alive but in other parts just seems to say that death may not be so bad and a little peaceful. Well, that is how I read it. It's all fine and good to live and try to get the most out of your life but sometimes you just have to call it quits. There is such a thing as too much of a good thing."

"How can you even say that?"

"Okay, going to prove my point. What was her name?"

"What?"

"What was your mothers name?"

"...."

"Too hard? I mean, I understand you were only with her minutes but I'm sure that old woman told you. How about that old woman's name? The woman that took you in and raised you, she taught you about magic and life and cared for you like you were her own child. What was her name?"

Talbot couldn't remember.

"Maybe you have a nickname for her? She raised you maybe you called her mama? Mother? Grandmother?"

"I - I - I don't remember." Talbot said quietly but then the anger over took him. "You did this! You made me forget!"

"I won't lie it is certainly in my power to erase a few memories but I didn't. Magic always has some sort of cost, life has a price to be paid and you'd put it off too long so you've started to lose other things to make up the bill."

"What are you talking about?"

"Immortality, if not balanced out just right, can wear away at the person. You've slowly been loosing your humanity and those rich emotions that made life worth living. You've lost the memories to those emotions. Can you even really remember the love that they had for you? I bet you only remember pain and fear when you mother died holding you. I bet you don't remember how much she loved you, she loved you a lifetimes worth in a few moments. The old woman adored you and played with you and showered you with love but all you remember was her death and her lessons. You didn't even get the emotion behind the lessons. How many people do you think you've forgotten completely? The emotional bonds people make between each other are powerful things and they help people get through the hard time but you've been cutting them off and refusing to make new one just for power. I mean, Redgrove was loyal to you and when he made a mistake you ripped his soul and used it for fuel. I mean your plan to end death requires you to kill people, its very nature was flawed. It collapses on in itself on logic alone."

"So, I did what I had to? I made mistakes." Talbot's voice was filled with anger as he spoke. "Is that wrong?"

"No, but the way you made those mistake was. It's one thing to forget to give someone their chance it's another thing to tell them they can trust you and then stab them. You used people without caring for what happened to them. You upset the natural balance for what you wanted not caring what others thought. You hurt people to reach your own goals. You were about to set yourself up as a god and rule over the world and would have chosen how people lived their lives. I don't know if you noticed this but all of that is things pretty much every religion and movement tells you not to do."

"So, is this supposed to be my own personal hell? Am I supposed to sit and think about what I have done?"

"I could have left you in the world and if you were lucky you'd be dead in an hour. Besides making the reapers angry, demons, magical organizations, angels, spirits, gods, and all sort of creatures are very upset with what you have done. I imagine a few of them would also like to get their hands or tentacles on you to know what you know and they would do anything to get that information." Talbot could swear he heard the voice snicker. "To answer your question: no, I don't plan to leave you here to think. That doesn't work with people like you. I can hear Karma calling me and ordering me to hand you and your cabal over to her. She's angry but she's usually angry at me anyway so I will just deal like I always do."

"Who are you?" Talbot asked the voice. "I saw those colored lights and I could sense your power."

"I am someone very angry at you. I'm the Keeper of the Dreamtime. I'm the source of the power of the Ley Line's of Earth and all other worlds. I am the First Born into this Universe. I am one of the Primordial. I watched the Universe form and I will watch it die. I am the embodiment of creation and birth as well as life. The Aboriginal people of Australia call me the Rainbow Serpent. The Ancient people of Egypt decided to call me Ouroboros. There are some people in Haiti that have come to know me as Ayida-Wedo. The First people to live and die in this Universe called me The One Who Shines In The Darkness. I am Life and I stand in judgement of you."

Two large eyes like glimmering diamonds appeared out of the darkness in front of Talbot. The eyes were beautiful and seemed to catch and reflect a light like no other and they seemed to stare right through Talbot and into his soul.

"Life?" Talbot questioned it. "Why would you of all people-?"

"You tore me away from Death. When your spell went off you twisted the veil and you kept me from this world too. You had dominion over life and death. I can forgive that, I really don't care, what I am really angry about is you hurt her, you hurt the person I love, you captured my wife and you hurt her. I'm not going to let you go because you hurt her and I'm more than little petty."

"You mean Death? Why would you care? Why would you of all the creatures in all of creation care about anyone much less Death? Why should anyone care? Why should anyone care about anyone standing in the way of their goals?!"

"Yes, I do mean Death." Life's voice was steady. "That's what I have been trying to explain to you, to think about other people. I see now that it's all lost on you. You can't think or even see other people's points of view. You don't care if people have to suffer so you can get your way, there have been despots and tyrants who thought like you and the world is better without them. Frankly I don't think I like the idea of you seeing her any time soon. Anyone else would kill you, she'd be merciful and end your lives but me....You won't be so lucky."

From out of the darkness the rest of Life's body formed. It wasn't human and it wasn't small. It was a snake with a white underbelly that was white as snow and the rest its body was covered in scales that shifted in color. The shining scales made it looked like a giant living rainbow whose colors shifted slowly across its body. At the tip of his tail was a silver ring engraved with symbols.

Life opened it's large jaws to reveal two huge pure white fangs.

Talbot had been surrounded by darkness for a very long time and now being in his own world of darkness made little difference. What happened to him next made all the difference in the world. Energy came out Life's mouth like a mist and touched Talbot. Talbot didn't die and Life didn't touch him. Life left a second later and didn't turn back as Talbot started to scream. He screamed and screamed and wouldn't stop screaming anytime soon.

Life left Talbot there alone but let Talbot feel every death on Earth, the death of every germ, every person, every animal, every fungus, every plant and anything else that lived and died. Talbot wouldn't die and wouldn't age or get sick or need food or need sleep. Life left him there to get a new insight on death and its importance. Talbot and every single member of the cabal were alone in their own little black worlds to experience the same thing until Life returned and Life had no intention on coming back any time soon.

It only took them minutes to realize that death could be a mercy, one they were denied because of their own denial of death.

Talk about irony.

Chapter 10: Deatz

Let's move to something less terrifying. Sofi and Valdis found themselves transported to the Realm of Death.

It wasn't what Sofi would have expected. It actually looked like a white office with a futuristic black metal desk with two black chair in front of it. On the opposite side of the room was a large tree, one lush and green with flowers blooming in every color. The tree sat in a clay pot that seemed out of place. The room was rather bare except for a few decorations on the white walls. A black sword decorated the wall behind the desk. As Sofi looked around she noticed that Valdis was standing with a stunned expression on her face as a woman stood behind her running a black brush through her hair. The woman was fixing the reaper's hair and putting it back into its pig tails.

"There that's better." Deatz said calmly before the brush vanished from her hand with a flashy shimmer.

Sofi noted that the woman was stunning especially in the elegant black dress wore whose skirt fell to her ankles. From her knee down there was a slit on the skirt that showed off her shapely leg. Her hair was smooth, long and black like a night without stars and her hair fell down her back like a gentle water fall. She wore red heels and her lips were painted a matching red. Honestly the red and the amber of her eyes were the only things keeping her from looking like a black and white photo.

"Sorry about how I look. Its date night I was pulled away when I was getting ready." Deatz answered a question that wasn't even asked. "I know you have a lot of questions and concerns but please wait a second. My husband will be along soon, he acted faster than I could when he grabbed the cabal. I'm sure he will be here soon. Don't worry you're in my realm so you don't have to worry you are safe here. Life currently has that cabal somewhere far, they're calling to me, begging for me but they're just out of my reach." Deatz didn't sound too concerned for them, like not concerned at all.

Deatz played with a silver ring on her finger, the ring had several symbols on it. She looked down at the ring and smiled.

There was a flash of light and the sound of thunder cracking as a rainbow snake appeared over head. Somehow the rainbow glowing snake floating in the air stuck out even more in a starch white environment. Life slithered through the air whirling around Deatz until he touched down on the ground besides her. Another quick flash of light and the snake turned into a tall man. He wore a long coat that waved behind him, the coat wasn't anything normal as it was a coat that seemed to be made out of light shaped into a coat around him. The coat almost looked to be alive as the colors danced around Life. He was a handsome man, thin with soft features. Life's diamond like eyes didn't focus on anything or anyone else but Deatz. A second later they grabbed one another and kissed each other in a passionate embrace, one of celebrating the fact that they were once again together. After a long moment they pulled away.

Worry coated Life's voice, "Are you okay?"

"I'm fine, you don't have to worry about me."

"You're my wife I think I get to worry."

"Oh, it wasn't that bad. You've been bound before."

"Yeah, and that wasn't bad because I was weak at the time and the stupid warlock did it wrong. It wasn't anything like what happened to you."

Truth be told it was bad. It hurt Deatz being torn away from the world, being reduced to your most basic state and having your power ripped from you. She knew Life was in a panic trying to get at her but the spell kept them separated with the Veil. She knew he was worried because she was worried when it happened to him and if given another moment he would have gone on a rampage like she did when he was bound.

Deatz watched him for a moment. "It's very sweet but I

promise you that I'm okay. Besides, remember the promise we made a long time ago? We promised that we would always find our way back to each other no matter what." Her milk white hand stroked his face as her nails turned candy red. She hadn't gotten to decorating her nail until that second.

Deatz smiled warmly at him, "Are you ready?"

"What?" Life blinked at her confused.

"Our date night."

"Don't change that subject."

"You promised you wouldn't wear that coat."

"You know that I put up the filters, normal people just see a coat a normal coat and the color depends on them."

"Your coat isn't something that helps with the romantic setting we are trying to build."

"I'll change." Life gave a sigh.

Life has just been wearing a pair of black slacks and a white shirt but he snapped his finger and his clothes changed. He wore a fancy blue dress shirt with gold buttons and a red tie. Life wore a pair of black and green bowling shoes with orange socks, he liked how the shoes looked and he thought they gave him a classy look but most people wouldn't agree. He wore a pair fancy black silk pants with a dark purple stitching forming whirling and swirling shapes and a few starbursts designs. The purple designs on the black pants were subtle and charming with a touch of whimsical. Finally he wore waist coat vest, it was just a vest version of his shimmering coat.

Deatz ran her fingers through his hair. "That's better." Deatz smirked. "I just wished you have some sense of color coordination."

"Says Miss-Black-and-White Movie."

"That's coming from the Technicolor Dream Coat? I don't think it means much."

While they had their playful banter Sofi collapsed to the floor. Sofi saw the truth so when it came to these two who choose how they appeared she saw right through that and to what they were. Deatz was death itself and her physical form wasn't something Sofi could really put into words at best it was a dark hazy thing. Deatz was bigger then she thought she was everywhere at once and nowhere at the same time. Sofi realized sometimes people thought they were alone when they died but really Death was there not causing peoples demise but she was there waiting. People didn't know when they were alone and crying she was there with them and she would have shown herself but people weren't ready for her. She created the reapers to help people get ready to meet with her. She was actually gentle like a cool breeze but could be strong like hurricane but choose not to when she could. She was everywhere and it was like she had wrapped herself around everyone and everything almost like a huge group hug.

    Life on the other hand was energetic and more like light but crazy fuzzy and blinding. He was like feeling the warmth of the sun on your face on a nice day or like stepping into a volcano when he wasn't friendly. Sofi could tell he usually tried to be friendly but it was harder to be friendly with people he thought were mean. He was spread out everywhere and nowhere like Deatz but he was interwoven into everything and sort of apart of everything. He too was there when people were alone he was always by Deatz and they were always there with people in bad times and good times but most people never saw them.

    The problem was that everything they were was being seen by Sofi and humans lacked the capacity to take all that in. It was like trying to see every thing on the planet Earth at the same time but much more.

    "Let me fix that." Life waved his hand.

    Sofi gasped as suddenly her powers stopped working and she saw and heard everything like everyone else did. "What did you do?"

    "Turned off the switch in your head. That's weird, very high perceptions that let you see past illusions and perceptions. That's much higher than normal ESP."

    "You can just turn off my abilities?" Sofi was shocked and

a little nervous now that she didn't know if he was lying. Sofi got up and looked at him.

"I'm old and know how mess with energy of every kind. It should be back in a few minutes." Life paused and turned to Deatz. "You changed the subject!"

Deatz couldn't help but let out a small giggle, "I was wondering how long it would take you."

"Okay, let finish this and head out to our date."

"I know you like dancing."

"I can hear the band playing our song." Life wrapped his arms around her. "Just think about it, us together by that little place by the ocean as the music plays. Dancing by the moon light." Life whispered to her swaying side to side.

"Sound romantic." Deatz smirked hearing his whispers.

"So let's hurry."

It almost felt like they had forgotten that Sofi and Valdis were there.

"Let's get to work then." Life pulled away from Deatz and waved his hand and with a shimmer Pax's appeared onto the floor.

Pax had been dead for some time now and his body had grown cold the moment that Deatz picked them up. There no pulling him back from the brink, no resuscitation at the last minute, he was gone. Valdis didn't sense a soul and assumed that as a reaper he understood what happened and had already moved on. Valdis wanted to break down and cry but she thought he wouldn't want that and tried to be strong. Valdis could only hope that he was at peace and happy. Both Sofi and Valdis found it hard to see him laying on the floor so motionless. Deatz walked over to him and Life stood on the other side. A large black bag appeared in her hands. Deatz opened the bag and searched through it. Deatz pulled out a ball of light.

"Pax?" Valdis spoke for the first time in moments. "That's his soul!"

"He's in the middle of crossing over." Deatz explained holding the orb in her hand gently. "I just grabbed it before it pushed all the way through into one of the afterlives."

Deatz put the soul right on Pax's chest and she and Life pushed down on it. The room was filled with light as the soul pressed through the body.

A loud gasp was heard as Pax jolted up.

"Welcome back Pax." Deatz greeted him with a smile.

"Thank you."

"I was dead and you where there." Pax looked around confused.

"It's my domain, I am everywhere, I am everything there."

Pax looked at his chest and found that his wounds were gone.

Life helped him get up, "There, good as new. I fixed everything and even your clothes, Great sitch work by the way."

"Thanks." Pax said still a little confused.

"You broke the spell and freed me." Deatz was happy to see him healthy. "I figured I owed you at least a do over."

"But, " Pax was worried. "don't these things have some problems? These things usually upsets the natural order of things."

"We are the order of things." Life told him frankly. "We handled the usual problems so don't worry about coming back wrong. There are a lot of things that are messy because of Talbot so no one will even care if we bring you back."

"Besides," Deatz smiled brightly. "the way we did it you wouldn't have come back if you really didn't want to."

Valdis couldn't bare it any more and jumped onto Pax and hugged. Sofi watched him for a second before she joined the hug.

Deatz looked over to Sofi, "Now, young lady. I have a warning to give you. There were plenty of people who saw what happened or will learn of it soon. Psychics, espers, magicians, and all sorts will be after you for your power."

"What?" Pax asked. "You can't just put her back in the world and hope for the best."

"There are rules." Deatz told him. "We can't just tell people to keep their hands off her."

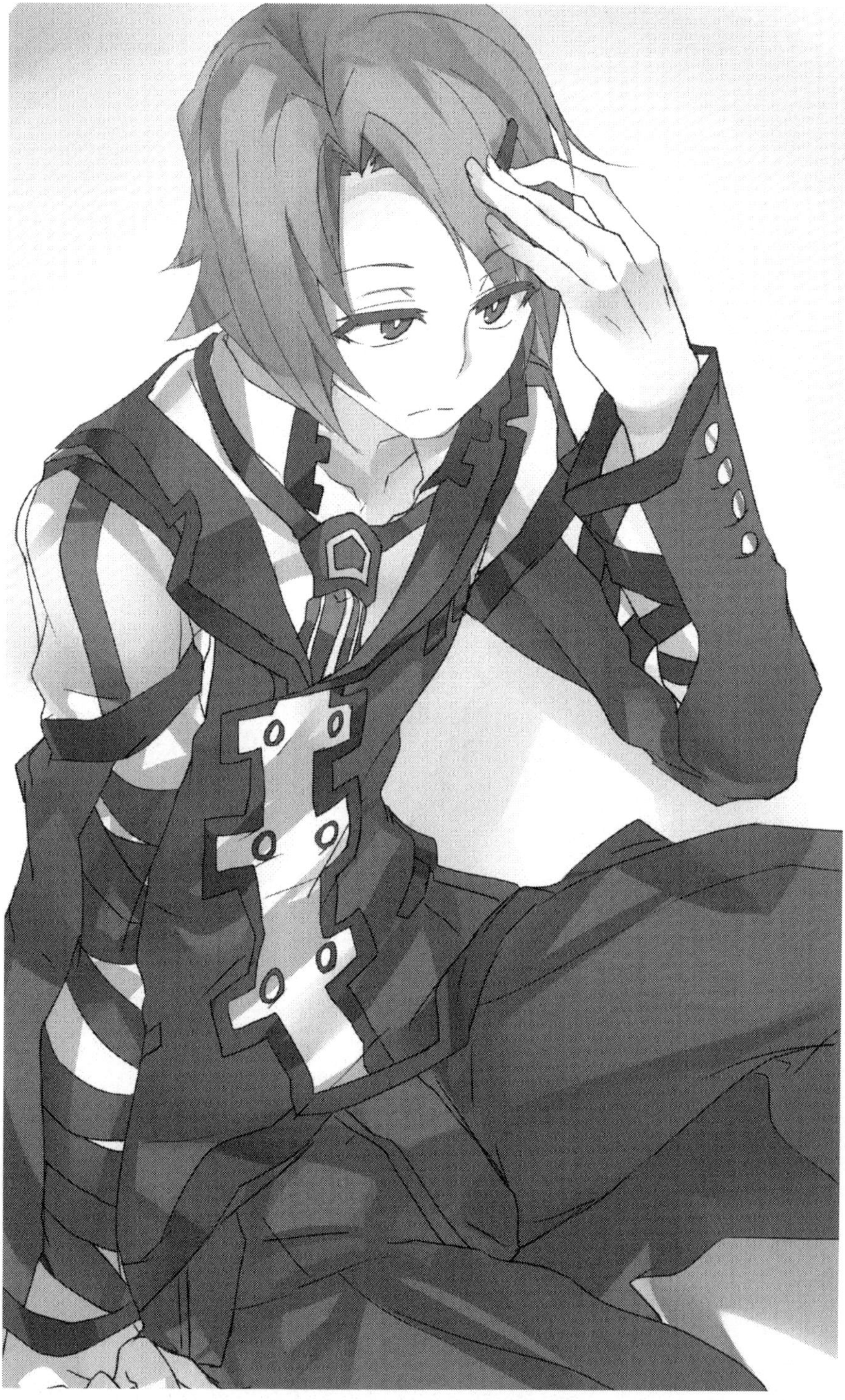

Maybe it was because he died only moments ago or it might have been everything that had happened in the day but he made a decision. "I'll protect her."

The room went silent.

"Okay." Life broke the silence.

Deatz rolled her eyes at her husband before she moved towards her reaper, "Pax, are you sure? If you become her guardian you will likely face untold dangers. It won't be easy. You will have to give up being a reaper."

Pax thought about it for a moment and he felt Valdis grip him tighter, "She needs help and it just looks like I'm the only one who can help."

"You sweet boy." Deatz sighed. "Okay, I usually require two weeks notice but I've waved that before. If you're sure about this then we have to bathe you in one of Life's pools."

"I'm sure." Pax said confident on his decision.

With that Life, Deatz and Pax vanished.

There wasn't a lot of time left and Valdis thought about everything. "Please take care of him."

"What?" Sofi questioned the sad looking reaper.

"I'm happy that Pax is alive and everything but if they do this he will be mortal and I won't get to see him. Pax can be sweet and he thinks too much and sometimes he doesn't see things that are in front of him. He will need someone to watch him."

"I promise I will." Sofi told her.

That was when the trio showed up from their quick trip into Life's realm. Pax was now fairly wet after being dunk into an actual pool.

"Okay, that should do it." Life told him.

"You're now half human and half reaper." Deatz explained it to him. "Normally I'd just turn you into human but since you will be her guardian I left some reaper. All your powers and limits will be cut down and you won't draw power from my realm. You will have to provide all your energy like any other person from Life's realm."

Pax used a towel to dry his hair. "Okay, I'm going have to eat to survive?"

"Yes, and you still have that wallet so use it." Pax nodded as he walked over to the girls the towel vanishing in his hands once he was dry.

"So are you okay with everything?" Pax asked her.

"I think." Sofi was honest. "I'm still a little surprised that Death is a girl."

"Sometimes I'm not." Deatz admitted.

Life added, "We can change gender whenever we want. We just choose to be these genders. There are cultures I just show up as girl just because."

"Same." Deatz gave a small shrug. "Sometimes its just easier to go with peoples expectations than explaining everything. Things like gender and appearance don't mean the same to us as they do to you. These forms we just happen to like the best."

Valdis walked up to Pax. "I guess this is good bye."

"I guess it is." Pax looked at his old friend. "I've just had the feeling that being a reaper wasn't really suited for me. Maybe this is. Maybe this is a chance for me to try and find what I am supposed to do and be."

"No, I understand. I think its better that you're out there finding yourself than being dead. I'm just going to miss you."

"Why are you going to miss him?" Deatz couldn't help but ask her reaper. "Your job is reaper of heroes and there aren't that many people that have the title of hero. You're not the only reaper of heroes. You got a lot of time free so I don't see why you can't go visit him any time you want when you're not working."

"...."

"You didn't think of that, did you?"

"No, I did not." Valdis didn't even bother to lie.

"Take a day off. I know we're busy but you've had a hard day and nearly got killed so you've earned it."

A smile warm smile spread across the reaper's face.

"Okay, if you will excuse us we have a nice dinner to get to and then off to dance." Life told the group. "Pax, you should get something to eat. If I may suggest try Italian food. Tomatoes are good and happy food. So have fun." Life smiled waving at the group and they just vanished.

"I hope they will be all right." Deatz crossed her arms looking at the now empty space.

"Yeah, they seem nice. I really hope Valdis works up the courage to tell Pax how she feels. I mean it's been centuries she really should get to it."

"Yeah, she really should."

"I know Pax isn't the smartest reaper but Valdis is pretty bright you'd think one of them would have thought to ask us what Sofi's power is about."

"It's been a busy day." Deatz looked over to him. "I'm sure they will find out soon enough."

"Well, Limerence is watching Veri for the night." Life offered his arm to her, "Will you come with me to a romantic night of dinner and dancing?"

"How is a girl going to refuse such an offer?" Deatz took his arm and the pair vanished leaving the room empty.

****

The trio found themselves in Italy just down the road of the Leaning Tower of Pisa. The sun was setting and it painted the sky with a wondrous orange glow.

"That was weird." Sofi put it bluntly.

"Yeah, I guess I'm your protector." Pax didn't know how good a job he could do, he had some power and knowledge gained from centuries of life as a reaper so that was pretty good. "I guess we should come up with a plan of what to do."

"Forget that for now." Valdis pulled at Pax's tie. "We have to get you something to eat. Italy is known for great food and we're here so lets get some food and then figure it out."

The world had gone back to normal. People came up with their own reason for why for a few minutes the sky went black. Most people quickly forgot it and it didn't even make the news.

The world carried on. Organizations figured out what had happened and about Sofi and soon would start making plans. Sofi wasn't worried, she was actually excited because she was finally getting a good look at the world she had so far only caught a glimpse of.

Valdis pulled Pax along and Sofi followed. Despite everything that happened she still had Pax in her life. Everything seemed right because of that. There was time to do all the things she wanted to do.

Pax wasn't sure about his life. As a reaper he had to collect the souls of those who died making mistakes and over time he felt he was worth as much as a mistake. He didn't see himself as anything special or as important even though he helped many people find their peace but that day he did find some worth. He found his worth not in saving the world but in saving his friends. Now, he had a clear purpose in protecting Sofi. He didn't know what his life would be like and to some extent that made it better. Instead of helping the already dead he got to help someone who was still alive. He wondered what else this new life would have for him.

As Valdis pulled Pax towards a nearest pizza place he thought he saw something. From the corner of his eyes he spotted a young with woman pale skin and brilliant red hair wearing a red dress that seemed to be made of red rose petals. She was sitting on a bench and next to her was a small boy wearing a simple brown shirt and blue jeans. His messy brown hair fell over his eyes but through his bangs tired gray eyes could be seen. His eyes were far older than his face, they were the eyes of someone who knew some secrets that most people wouldn't dare think were true.

They both sat on the bench eating a frozen treat called gelato.

The girl was known as Limerence. She looked over to the boy and said, "Those are the reapers that saved mom today?"

The boy who was called Veri nodded and simply said, "Yeah."

"And that's the girl that people are talking about."

"Yes." Veri licked his gelato.

"Do you get the feeling that our uncle is playing with them?"

"Yes." Veri still didn't turn to her.

"So what do you think is going to find them next?"

Veri turned to his sister and said one word, "Trouble."

They say that the future is unknown and for the most part it is. It is probably better that it is. But the future did have a few promises, trouble would soon come but despite that there was also the chance of happiness. In the end you can only hope that there is that chance and that when it comes you take it.

Life is short and it is better to live it when you can because you don't know when it will end. Still endings are things not to be afraid of, endings can also be the start of something new.

Afterword

Hello dear readers I am Ivan Navi and thank you for reading. You can also call me something else if you like, the Author or the Narrator will work. I do enjoy being called by titles. First of all, or possibly second, I want to thank you for taking the time to read my book, I hope you enjoyed it. This is first book I've gotten published so I'm very excited about all this. I've liked stories and telling stories since I was a kid so writing stories just felt like the natural thing for me to do. I honestly just love writing so to be able to do something I love like this is just a great experience.

Some of you might be asking why I wrote a story on reapers. The idea is very interesting to me, after all these are figures that are in cultures around the world. Some of these figures are scary and some are really friendly. The fact that there are so many differences between these figures that all serve the same end is just so amazing to me. I just loved seeing all the different interpretations of these figures and what they stand for.

This is why I love mythology and folklore, it gives me such a grand view of how people think and what ideas they hold dear. Just take the reapers as an example. The stories of the Grim Reaper were meant to be scary so people would be more careful, to treasure life while they have it. Stories about Valkyrie were meant to express the idea that there was glory and peace after a death in battle for brave warriors. It's the ideas that we share with others that say who we are. Some people wanted people to cautious and some wanted people to have a reward. I guess that brings up what I want to do with my ideas. I want to share this story with everyone. I think I will just let you come to your own conclusions beyond that. I know myself well enough to know that I don't know myself well enough to really know me.

That wasn't my attempt to sound profound or anything I just know I am still trying to figure myself out. Life is more interesting with a bit of mystery and I do like interesting things. That is what I hope to bring to you all with my stories, something interesting. There is plenty to work within this world I have in my stories. In this world there are stories to be told not only about reapers but also about Life and Death, their minder, a time traveler, dragons, monsters, gods, spirits, ghosts, creatures from other worlds, heroes, villains and much more. I hope I can share all the stories I've had running in my head for a while.

Finally I would like to thank everyone whose helped me along the way, my friends and my family. Thanks to my dad for being supportive in his own way. Thanks to my friends for keeping me going and getting me out of trouble whenever trouble seems to find me. Thanks to Yosuke Imagawa for giving the chance to write this. Honestly, thanks to everyone whose made this possible. Thanks to the illustrator Kiyoichi who made all the wonderful illustrations that have shown up in this book and the cover. Of course, thanks to you dear reader for taking the time to read this. I hope I get another chance to write another one of these novels and I hope you will enjoy that one too.

-Ivan Navi

Printed in Great Britain
by Amazon